USA TODAY BESTSELLING AUTHOR

Dale Mayer

the Haven

JAXON 03

JAXON: THE HAVEN, BOOK 3
Beverly Dale Mayer
Valley Publishing Ltd.

Copyright © 2025 Beverly Dale Mayer

All rights reserved. Except for use in any review, the reproduction or utilization of this work in whole or in part by any electronic, mechanical, or other means, now known or hereafter invented, including xerography, photocopying and recording, or in any information storage or retrieval system, is forbidden without the written permission of the publisher.

This is a work of fiction. Names, characters, places, brands, media, and incidents either are the product of the author's imagination or are used fictitiously. Any resemblance to actual events, locales, or persons, living or dead, is entirely coincidental.

ISBN-13: 978-1-778867-40-8
Print Edition

Books in This Series:

Timber, Book 1

Burke, Book 2

Jaxon, Book 3

Sterling, Book 4

About This Book

Jaxon, regaining his physical health but still haunted by the emotional scars of an unwanted impending divorce, finds solace working at the Haven, where he feels welcomed and at home, at least for now. However, his sense of peace is shattered when Tiffany arranges for the arrival of llamas in distress, and he discovers that Keisha, his ex, is the one transporting them.

Stunned by the encounter, Jaxon struggles to maintain his composure, but his priority remains the animals in need. As he navigates the unexpected tension, he resolves to protect his heart, even if it means being overly cautious. Keisha's sister had been a sore point between them before, and that hadn't changed.

As Jaxon and Keisha begin to communicate and to address their past, a new threat emerges involving her sister, posing unforeseen dangers. Amid the suspense, a heartwarming love starts to rekindle between them, offering hope and healing in the face of adversity.

Sign up to be notified of all Dale's releases here!
https://geni.us/DaleNews

PROLOGUE

ABOUT A WEEK later Timber strode up the front yard and watched as the trailer backed up to the paddock. He looked over at Tiffany and asked, "Are you ready for this?"

"No, probably not," she admitted, "but … alpacas and llamas apparently will be part of the family from now on. They are just some of the animals we'll be looking after."

As he walked into the paddock and saw that the trailer was full, he smiled because it was either smile or cry, and he was not one to cry very easily, at least not in public. Yet the animals always made him feel such emotions. These animals were horribly thin and desperately in need of shearing and some love and attention.

He looked over at Jimmy, who had driven them here. Timber's tone bleak, he asked, "Is this all of them?"

"It is, and two of them may not even make it," Jimmy warned. "I'm not sure what to say about them."

"No, I don't know either," he murmured, "but let's get going."

At that, another woman walked up.

Timber looked over at her and frowned. "Keisha?"

Keisha nodded. "Hey, Timber. How are you doing?"

"What are you doing here?"

"I heard an extra load of animals was headed this way

when I was talking to Tiffany," she explained, "so I thought I would come lend a hand."

"You're always welcome. You do know Jaxon is here, right?"

She looked over at him and asked, "Is that a problem?"

"Not for me, as long as it's not for you."

"Nope, not a problem for me," she stated. "He's my ex for a reason."

"I know," he replied, "but I also know that it's not an easy ex."

"There's no such thing as easy exes," she declared. She came around to the side and stopped when she saw the animals. "Dear God," she whispered.

"Yeah, I hear you," Tiffany muttered at her side. "Let's get to work."

At that, a shout came from the other side, and Jaxon walked over. "I saw the trailer come in and thought you could use an extra hand. What are we doing?" Then he turned, and his eyes widened when he saw Keisha. "Hey," he muttered, as he pushed back his hat. "I didn't know you would be here."

"I didn't know I would be here either, until I heard so many animals were in need," she shared. "I came to help Tiffany. You got a problem with that?"

Everybody else ignored the hint of challenge in her voice. Jaxon stared at her, then over at Timber. "No problem here. Animals first."

And, with that, they all got down to work.

CHAPTER 1

J AXON HILLSBOROUGH STEPPED into the paddock quietly and steadily, watching the animals as they shied away from him. The new arrivals were expected to be … jittery. They'd been processed, but he wasn't sure that decisions had been made on any of their care yet. As he stood here studying their conditions, he winced, seeing how much time and attention was required to get them back to full health. As he considered each of them, Keisha walked around the side. The moment she saw him, she literally came to a stop. And then, with a seriously controlled movement, she stepped forward and said hello in a low tone.

He nodded at her but didn't say anything. It shouldn't have shocked him so to see her here. After all, she was a veterinarian, and more than one would be in great need at the Haven.

"I guess I should have warned you."

He shrugged. "Doesn't matter, does it?" He shook his head. "You're here for the animals, not me, so what difference does it make?" She let out her breath in a long slow exhale. He remembered her doing that a lot when she needed patience, and, with a nod toward her, he muttered, "I've got to get back to work." And he turned and walked away.

"We don't have to be enemies," she called out.

He stopped and looked back at her. "I'm nobody's enemy," he stated, "but we sure aren't friends." And, with that, he stepped out of the paddock and left. Maybe it wasn't the best thing for him to say, but the hurt was real and the pain still too raw.

As far as *he* was concerned, she was his wife. So far as *she* was concerned, he'd been temporary, a fling of sorts. And that was something he wasn't sure he would ever get over. He walked into the kitchen and poured himself a quick cup of coffee. As he looked out the kitchen window, he saw Dwight on the back deck, hand-feeding a squirrel. Jaxon grinned.

When Timber joined him just minutes later, Jaxon asked him, "Is that the infamous Dodger?"

"Sure is. He's been picking favorites, depending on the time of day." Timber faced him and asked, "You doing okay, Jaxon?"

He shrugged. "I will be."

"Good," Timber noted. "We need her help right now."

"Of course you do," he agreed, with half a smile, "and she'll be a big help."

"She's not staying, you know?"

He shrugged. "It's your place, man, not mine." And he tried really hard to keep his tone as neutral as he wanted to, but he knew from the look on Timber's face that he'd failed.

Timber Woodland was nothing if not exceptional at reading people. He was a SEAL turned military medic, and he was a force on wheels, until his accident. Still, he'd managed to get his shit together and to create a sanctuary for all of them—abused people and animals alike. Jaxon realized his outburst had been totally misplaced. He closed his eyes briefly and added, "It was just a shock."

"Of course it was. I'm sorry that happened. I didn't

know she was coming either."

"She did just say she should have let me know."

"But, of course, the animals were on her mind, not you." Seeing Jaxon's expression, Timber winced. "I'm sorry. That … would have hurt some more."

Jaxon looked over at his friend, smirked, then sighed. "Just because I need to let go doesn't mean it's easy to."

"It's never easy to let go, particularly if you're not ready," Timber shared, studying his friend as he poured a cup of coffee for himself. He looked back at him and added, "I wouldn't want to lose you over this."

"If she's not staying, you won't lose me," he declared, with a shrug. "Besides, one day I'll have to make a decision about what to do with my life."

"You don't have to do it today," Timber declared. "You've had enough shocks for the day."

"And the animals?"

"They've been processed, and Tiffany is working up a schedule. She'll have to do a bit of research," he noted.

"Research? For what?"

"She hasn't really worked with llamas before," he conceded, with half a smile. "That's not exactly what we thought we would be dealing with."

"It's easy to see how a homeowner with good intentions could get into trouble though," Jaxon pointed out, as he looked over at Timber. "I don't feel as if these guys were deliberately abused. More likely neglected through igno-rance."

"I agree. I think they tried to do something good for the animals and failed. Like so many things in life, it's just not that easy to do what you want to do all the time, and all of it takes money and resources."

Jaxon nodded, then frowned at his friend. "And how are your resources?" he asked, with a note of humor in his tone. "You grew very quickly here."

Timber frowned, then snorted. "Yeah, I sure did, and that wasn't exactly planned either. Just seeing how much work has been done here, it's embarrassing for me to admit that my original plan was to do it all myself. Thankfully everybody showed up, and it took on a life of its own. I never expected all you guys to volunteer so much of your time."

"Sure, but, as it turns out, you are providing something we need far more than paychecks right now," he shared. "A place to land and a place to work in a community where we share more than a love of animals, all while we figure out what we'll do with the rest of our lives."

"And was Keisha part of the reason that you needed time and space to figure that out?" Timber asked.

"That's some of it," he agreed, nodding his head. "I wanted something and thought I had it. So, I came home full of joy—even though I was broken and worried about what kind of shape I would be in for the rest of my life—but I still hoped for the best," he stated. "Then reality hit me, and apparently I'm not good enough anymore," he said, with a groan, as he stared out the window. Then he just shrugged it off. "I can't blame her. I didn't come home healthy and whole."

"None of us did," Timber noted. "None of us did."

"That doesn't mean she understood it though."

"Or did she need you to go off and to get your shit together first?" Timber suggested.

"Probably," he agreed in a half-cheerful, half-bitter tone. He put down his empty coffee cup and added, "I'll head over to the bunkhouse and see if I can find something to do."

"I'm sure there's plenty," Timber replied, his tone calm. "Just please"—he turned to him—"please don't run."

"Wasn't planning on it," Jaxon declared, "but I'm not sure I'm showing up for dinner." And, with that, he turned and walked out.

⌒

AFTER JAXON LEFT, Toby stepped forward and muttered, "I guess Keisha appearing here threw him for a loop, didn't it?"

"It sure did," Timber confirmed. "And it'll take him a little time to recover."

"Any idea how long they were married?"

"Only a few months before he was deployed. I'm not sure exactly what happened, but apparently it didn't last through him getting back home."

"That's tough," Toby said, "but not unheard of. I swear to God, most of the guys here have dealt with some version of the same thing."

"That isn't anything we want to tell Jaxon, and that's definitely not what he needs to hear right now."

"No, it sure isn't." Toby swore. "Damn, I feel bad as I kind of like her as a person."

"I know, and, according to Tiffany, she's good people."

"So, what the hell went wrong?"

"I'm not sure anything has to go wrong, as much as people go wrong. He told me how he came back damaged, not whole, and, as far as Jaxon's concerned, this was the end result."

"And yet she's here helping animals that aren't whole," Toby pointed out. "So it doesn't seem to me as if that's necessarily true."

"Maybe not, but you also have to understand that what we hear versus what they say? Well, … sometimes that's two different things."

Toby nodded. "If people would just honestly communicate …"

"Communicating would be lovely," Timber agreed, with a smile in Toby's direction. "But again, communicating *well* is a whole different story. I'll head over to the bunkhouse, just to keep an eye on him."

"You do that," Toby replied. "Jaxon's been good to have around."

"I know. He pitches in and does anything we need done. He's really skilled too …" Timber looked back to where Jaxon had gone. "Yet I can tell he's hurting."

"Yeah, you're not kidding," Toby agreed. "Yet it looks as if the reason for that is right out there in the barn."

Timber turned to him and nodded. "We need to help him, along with these animals."

"If we can just keep him moving along, with Keisha around here too, sometimes without any blowups, maybe they can find a way to just be social," Toby suggested. "They don't have to be friends, but it would be nice if they could at least be … *polite*, at least rub shoulders in the same setting and not have everybody else uncomfortable because of their tension."

"I would love it if that could work out," Timber replied, "but it's not up to us."

JAXON STOOD ON the deck, out of sight and just past the

equipment, and had heard it all. He realized what an imposition all of this would be and swore again that he was in this situation. It's not what he thought he was coming home to, and it certainly wasn't what he had thought would be here at the Haven, but this was Timber's place, and Timber sure needed the help. So, if one of them had to go, it would be Jaxon again. Timber needed another veterinarian, so Jaxon was the surplus worker here.

And, with that thought, he headed straight toward the bunkhouse, wondering what he could do and what he should do, considering the circumstances. It was a hard-enough thing to be sorting through, but, in truth, he didn't have a whole lot of choices right now.

When he got to the bunkhouse, Timber wasn't far behind him. Jaxon didn't say anything or mention that he'd overheard part of the earlier conversation. Jaxon just got to work. A couple of the other men looked over at him. They didn't say anything, but a few questioning glances were exchanged between them and Timber. Thankfully nobody brought up Keisha, and Jaxon got to work on his own. When his phone rang off the hook, he looked down to see a number he hadn't seen in a very long time. He picked up the call. "Hey, Rose. How are you doing?"

"I'm doing okay," she responded in that same bright cheerful voice. "How are you doing?"

"I'm fine," he murmured, "but I'm at work right now."

After a moment of hesitation, she asked, "But are you actually working?"

"What do you mean by that?" he asked, with a silent groan. "You know I'm working."

"I know you're working, or at least you're keeping busy, but I don't know that you're actually working."

"Which shouldn't make any difference to you. What's the matter?"

"It's just … we haven't done the signatures on that divorce of yours yet."

"Right, yeah, well, … she's here right now, so I don't know what to tell you."

"What do you mean, she's there?"

"Just what I said. She's here, at the Haven. She came in to see about a load of animals."

"That's an interesting twist."

"Not really. I don't think anything about it is interesting," he snapped.

Rose sighed. "We don't have to go through with this right now."

"What do you mean, we don't have to?" he asked, with a snort. "Nothing is left of my marriage, and she's the one who filed for divorce."

"I know, but you could talk to her."

"What good will that do?" he asked, with yet another snort. "It's not as if talking to her has ever done any good so far."

"I don't know what to say about that because it seemed to me that you two were really good at communicating, … right up until you weren't."

"Yeah, well, things were great until they weren't," he declared. "Now either send me the damn paperwork, and I'll go over it, or don't." When an odd silence came from the other end, he knew what a jerk he had been. "Look. I'm sorry. I'm not trying to snap at you, but it was a bit of a shock when she just showed up here, out of the blue."

"Yeah, it's weird that she did that."

"Why?" he asked.

"I just had a phone call with her lawyer this morning, and he wanted to know why you hadn't signed the papers."

"That might explain why she showed up then," he muttered, pushing his hair off his face.

"Maybe."

Jaxon heard the odd note in her tone and asked, "What?"

"It could be that, or else she's looking to see if this is still what you guys want."

"I don't know what she's up to," he snapped. "I didn't start this process, so if she's here because she's pushing for signed paperwork, that's on her." He took a deep breath. "Just send the damn stuff, and I'll take a look at it." When he disconnected, he stood here, glaring out at the paddocks around him. None of the men behind him said anything, but he felt their gazes boring into the back of his head and knew that they had overheard his part of the discussion. Bad call on his part. He should have been more careful about having personal phone calls around here when others were nearby. Too late for that now.

He shrugged irritably and returned to the work at hand. He wasn't sure what he was supposed to do. He wasn't sure about anything right now. So, the only thing he could do was focus on the work right in front of him now. When his phone rang again, he looked down at the screen and refused the call.

Timber laughed nearby. "I should try that with my lawyers."

"This one wasn't the lawyer," he snapped and then groaned. "Sorry, that's a completely different ... *issue*." He dragged out the word, making a lisping sound.

"Wow, ... you've got a couple of those chasing you."

"I do and wish I didn't, but I wouldn't categorize it as *chasing* exactly," he clarified, with a shrug. "What can I say? Life got complicated very quickly."

"Anything that's really ugly?"

"Not that I know of," he muttered, turning to face him.

"I just don't want anyone to get blindsided," Timber replied, his gaze piercing as he studied Jaxon.

"You're thinking about Burke?"

"Like I said …"

"Nope, nothing to be blindsided over here. I don't think it's anything like what Shirley was going through—or Burke or even you and Tiffany," Jaxon noted. "I don't know who the hell this person is, but they keep calling me."

"Maybe that's something you should check out," Timber suggested.

"I would, but that means acknowledging them," Jaxon pointed out, "and I'm not prepared to do that. They just keep calling, and I keep disconnecting and not letting them through. It's just spam, as far as I'm concerned."

"They might be spam."

Jaxon faced Timber, his facial expression hard.

Timber smiled and shrugged. "Fine, I'll leave it be."

"Yeah, right," Jaxon muttered, with a snort. "You'll leave it for five minutes, and then you'll be hounding me again."

"Maybe," Timber conceded, "but I'm not trying to hound you though."

Jaxon sighed. "Look, … it's been a tough day."

"Got it." Timber nodded. "I get that, but, if you still care that much for Keisha, and it's sending you all over the place, it might be something that's worth fighting for."

"How do you fight for something you didn't even know you'd lost?" he asked, staring at him. "I lost it way before I ever got home, so what do I do with that?" he exclaimed, followed by a sigh.

"You could always talk to her, see what's going on, see if anything is still there anymore. Until you talk to her, you don't know the full story."

"There isn't any need. She made that very clear when she had me served with divorce papers," he declared, "and, if I thought anything was left, I would have fought, but the divorce papers mean something completely different, and I am not going back to where I was."

CHAPTER 2

TIFFANY LOOKED OVER at Keisha and asked, "Are you sorry you came?"

Keisha shrugged. "Had to happen sometime," she muttered.

"Are you doing okay though?"

"Sure, of course I'm doing okay," she replied, with a bright smile for her friend. "I knew this time was coming and something that was needed. We move in the same circle, so it would happen eventually anyway. I just wasn't thinking that today would be the day."

"Of course not, and it didn't need to be."

"No, but today you needed help, and I won't let life stop me from doing the things that need to be done, and today we had animals that needed help," she explained. "No need to make a fuss now. It's all good."

"I appreciate the help."

"I know you do and so do these animals." Keisha gently stroked the neck of a very hot llama. "We really need to get shearers out here."

"I've made several phone calls, but they are a dying breed."

Keisha winced but nodded. "I know that he probably won't volunteer, but Jaxon is a pretty-decent shearer."

"Where on earth would he have learned that?"

"He was raised on a ranch, and they always had sheep, as well as a few other curiosities. His father would never pay for the proper people to come by and take care of things, so Jaxon used to do the job for them."

Tiffany looked over at the animals and frowned.

"I know I'm making it sound as if he would do a terrible job, but honestly, he's pretty decent."

"And you've seen it?"

"I've seen him at work. I'm not sure he would appreciate what I'm saying though."

"Of course not," she said, with a nod. "It would help if he volunteered."

"Sure, but, if he doesn't know what's needed, he can't volunteer," she pointed out, "and, if you don't say something to him, he won't know."

"I can ask him," Tiffany noted. "Absolutely I can ask him. I did pick up some decent shears, but I've never used them before. Plus, I'm not sure I can manhandle these guys as it is."

"Probably not." Keisha frowned at them and then smiled. "Obviously it'll be more than a one-person job, so I guess that would be him and me," Keisha pointed out, with a sigh, "but, if you tell him that, he'll immediately say no."

"You don't know that," said a man behind them, his tone hard.

Wincing, Keisha turned to see Jaxon standing there, glaring at her.

He asked, "What is it you think I can do?"

"We can't get a shearer," Tiffany stated immediately, "and Keisha mentioned you're a decent shearer."

His eyebrows shot up. "That's a plus," he muttered. "Spilling secrets, are we?" He walked over, took a look at the llamas, and nodded, ignoring Keisha. "These coats need to come off," he declared, turning to Tiffany. "You sure you couldn't get anybody? These mats won't make for an easy job. A pro would be better to not stress out the animals."

"True. However, we're not trying to save the wool. In this case, I see wool breaks all over anyway. Instead of long healthy strands, the wool has breaks in the fibers, likely due to stress and diet changes."

"I agree," he said, taking a closer look at the animals, their mouths open from the heat that was already tormenting them. He frowned as he studied them and added, "It won't be pretty."

"I don't need pretty," Tiffany stated. "I just need the animals cooled down to reduce heat stress at this point."

"Well, in that case, have you got shears?"

"I picked up a good set a while back when I found out what Timber was planning out here," she shared, "and brought them with me from the clinic." She pointed toward them.

He walked over and took a look, then nodded, plugged them in, took a good look around the shop, and muttered, "I'll have to get more wiring done in here. We have an outlet here, but more are still in the works. If you'll do this on a regular basis, we'll need better access."

"Yeah, we can talk more about that as soon as we get the animals in," she noted. "It usually takes a little bit of a trial run before everybody can figure out exactly what's needed in a place like this anyway."

He didn't say anything but walked over to the first llama and took a closer look at it. "It's just you and me, bud," he whispered, "but, with a little cooperation, we can get through this."

Of course, cooperation was asking a lot from a stressed and overheated animal, but, even as he started, the animal seemed to calm down. Jaxon managed to get the animal down on one side, bringing the shears up through the belly. It was almost magical to watch, and Keisha couldn't take her gaze off him.

When he struggled a little bit, keeping the animal calm while he did their legs, he looked up and announced, "A little help would be nice."

Keisha immediately jumped into action and held the llama, keeping it still in order for him to get to the places that he needed to reach, before rolling over the llama and completing the other side.

By the time he was done, he stood back and helped the animal to its feet, cleaning up the animal's neck in the process. "It certainly wasn't a three-minute pro job," he admitted, as he looked at the animal with satisfaction, "but it's better than what he had."

And, indeed, the animal slowly stopped panting. With that first one done, they went to work on the rest, and by the time they were all done, Keisha was shaking.

"I didn't think it would be that much work," Keisha admitted with a hard sigh, as she stepped back.

"It wasn't a lot of work for us," Jaxon clarified briskly. "It was nothing compared to what it was for them."

She nodded. "Very true," she muttered, knowing he struggled with her being here anyway. She looked over at him and shared, "I wasn't trying to avoid you or to pin you in place."

He looked at her briefly, cleaned off the shears, and started to walk away. "Doesn't matter now if you did or not," he noted, "as it didn't work either way." And, with that, he stepped outside.

Tiffany raced behind him and called out, "Hey, Jaxon."

He pivoted and almost snapped, "What?"

"Take it easy now," she said, with a smile. "I just want to thank you. Those animals were really suffering from the heat in there."

"Yeah, they sure were," he conceded. "You'll have to keep them shorn regularly."

"And I'm okay with that," she replied, and then she laughed. "You better tell Timber that too."

"He knows it." Jaxon gave her a quiet smile. And, with that, he turned and walked back to the bunkhouse.

CHAPTER 3

J AXON FELT STRESS in areas he hadn't expected from that shearing event, and his heart still raced from the physical effort he had expended, combined with the fear of hurting the animals. Although he had done it before, it wasn't exactly an easy job, and it took years to build up the kind of skills and tolerance to not hurt the animals, which was all he really wanted. He was just glad the job was over.

As he stepped into the bunkhouse, several of the men smiled at him.

"Hey, how did that go?" asked one of them.

"A little rough," Jaxon admitted, as he rubbed his shoulder, his limp noticeable now.

Immediately their smiles fell away.

"Right, even though we're recovering …" muttered another one.

Jaxon nodded. "Even though we're recovering, it doesn't mean we're quite recovered, but, hey, if I can do something over here, let me know," he offered, now rubbing his temples.

"Maybe go have a shower?" one suggested.

"I would love a shower, but the day isn't done." Seeing the smirks on most of their faces, he stopped, looked down at his watch. "Wow."

"Yeah, exactly. The day may not be done, but it's pretty-dang close," one of the men stated, with chuckles all around.

Jaxon frowned, looked at his watch again, and shrugged. "Maybe I will just grab that shower then," he said reluctantly.

"Get some heat on that shoulder and see about getting off your feet and taking off the prosthetic," suggested one of the men. "It was a good thing you did, but it'll also impact your joints."

"I hope not," he muttered. "I have to get in to see Kat in the next couple days anyway."

"And she's doing you a hell of a solid in terms of helping you out as it is. So she won't take it kindly if you abuse her hard work."

He looked over at him and smiled. "She knows the hardware gets abused. It's just a fact of life when you're up on your feet all the time," Jaxon pointed out. "I don't think very much would upset her."

"And that is a huge plus," Toby agreed, entering the bunkhouse, a smile on his face, "because she's really been helping a lot of you guys, hasn't she?"

"Yeah, she sure has," Jaxon confirmed. "She's good people."

"Indeed, and that makes a big difference in terms of the work we do too," Toby added.

"Are you sure?" Jaxon quipped, with half a smile in his direction. "Kind of seems you guys are just happy to have as much help as you can get."

"Oh my God, we absolutely are," he muttered.

"And you're staying, right?" one of the other men asked Toby. "No running? By the looks of it, you've been on the run for some time now. It doesn't help."

"Yeah, Toby. What's the deal with that?" asked another.

"For me, I'm just done trying to go anywhere else," Toby shared. "Here at the Haven, I found a place where I would really like to stay. So talks are on about building a house up on a small piece of land nearby. Same deal for Dwight. We've been friends for decades. Would love to settle down close by."

The men stared at him, and Toby nodded. "This is home for me. I just need to get a piece of land and build on it," he added. "I don't know how much land might be available, but, if it's something you're interested in, you might want to talk to Timber about it."

"Talk to Timber?" one of the men repeated, immediately stepping forward, looking from Toby to the others. "I could sure use that. I won't be much of a hand at building a whole house on my own," he acknowledged, "but, if anybody wants help with theirs, and could give me hand on mine, I would be right there with it."

"I think that's what the plan is for several of us already," Toby confirmed, with half a smile. "And hopefully, between those of us who are here looking to have a place to call home, we can end up with something that's livable."

"More than livable," declared Timber, as he stepped in as Toby went out. "*Just livable* is what we were doing now," he pointed out, looking from one man to the next, all around at them. "However, *thriving* is what we need."

"How do we get in on that deal?"

"You already are. Anybody who is interested in land just needs to let me know. I don't know how much will be up for negotiation, but it'll all come from the original land owner. The price could be right, but the agreement is, the land is not for commercial development. Each is intended to be for a small plot of land to build yourselves a little home of your own, so you have your own space."

One of the men nodded. "That would be a huge opportunity," he said.

"There's still a price tag attached," Timber reminded them all, "and again I don't know what that'll look like yet. We're just really hoping that it's something reasonable."

"I'm in," added one of the other men in the far back corner.

Jaxon turned to look at him and smiled. "I can see this would be perfect for you."

"I think it's perfect for anybody who's still looking for a place to call home. So many of us have lost so much that just the promise of getting a little something back, to own and to be free from all the baggage, … that's amazing."

"Of course it is," Timber agreed. "Again, no promises though. We're dealing with the current owner on these plots."

"Understood," he replied, with a quiet smile, then went back to doing some high-quality woodwork.

"What are you building?" Timber asked.

"Built-in dressers and cabinets," he said, without lifting his head.

"That's a hell of a job."

"Yeah, … it would be nice to do this work full-time," he shared. "And maybe I'll look at it on a more professional basis when I get there. So, if I thought there was a place I could call home and not get chased away, I would be there in a heartbeat."

"I'll put your name down," Timber noted. He exchanged a quiet smile with another man and then looked over at some of the others. "Some of you guys have places to go to, right?"

"Some of us do, and some of us did," one of the men pointed out, "until we came back to find that the places we thought we had weren't as solid and secure as we had hoped."

"Right, I hear you there," Jaxon acknowledged, working hard to keep the bitterness out of his tone but failing. "It's hard when you come back and when you think you've got everything you could possibly want again, only to realize that you didn't really have it in the first place." Just then the big bell for dinner rang, and he started over to the kitchen.

One of the men came up behind him and asked, "Are you sure you don't want to shower first?"

"If I take a shower, you guys will eat all the food," he quipped, with a smile in his buddy's direction.

"Well, … maybe," he acknowledged, "but we might prefer it if you got a shower first."

"Don't really give a crap," Jaxon muttered. "I'll have a shower after I eat."

As he entered the dining area, some of the guys were joking about the new animal in the woods. He ignored them and walked over and grabbed some food and sat down with the intention of eating, only to be interrupted by a sudden silence all around, as two women stepped into the dining room.

Most of the seating was already gone.

Tiffany walked over and sat down beside Timber.

He looked over at her and asked, "How are the llamas and alpacas doing?"

"Now that they're sheared and cleaned up a little bit, they're doing pretty well," she stated, as she nodded at Jaxon. "Thanks for that."

He shrugged. "I already told you there was no need to

thank me. It's all for the animals."

"I know," she replied, "but it was still appreciated."

He didn't say anything and just kept eating. When the other men started to shuffle ever-so-slightly, Jaxon looked up and realized that Keisha still stood there with her plate, not sure where to sit.

One of the men immediately pointed beside Jaxon and told her, "There's room there."

She hesitated, then shrugged. "There might be room," she said in a joking tone, "but that doesn't mean there's a welcome."

Jaxon stiffened at that and glared at her. "Maybe not with that attitude." And, with that, he shoveled the last of the food off his plate and into his mouth. Then he got up, took his dishes to the kitchen, rinsed them, and placed them in the dishwasher.

He thanked Dwight for dinner, and, without another word, he walked out.

CHAPTER 4

TO SAY DINNER was an awkward affair was to put it mildly. Then again Keisha knew it was her fault. One, she hadn't warned Jaxon, and, two, he was right. She hadn't come across with a great attitude when she first walked in to have dinner, looking for a place to sit. Instead of taking it good-naturedly and grabbing whatever spot was available, she had made a point of saying that she wasn't welcome, which had immediately set off Jaxon. He had been a rough stranger since she'd arrived, and she wasn't sure she expected anything different—or that she deserved anything different.

She sat here, appreciating that Tiffany was trying to keep the conversation going in the hopes that some of this would smooth over. However, since Keisha had made the mistake in the first place, she wasn't feeling up to increasing the damage. As soon as she finished eating, she thanked Timber and turned to Tiffany. "Tiff, if you don't need me anymore, I'll head out."

"I'll walk you out," she offered immediately.

As Keisha left, several of the men called out their good-byes. Keisha smiled, gave them a wave, took one last look at the animals, then walked over to her truck.

Tiffany smiled at her friend and fellow veterinarian. "I really appreciate the help today."

"I'm glad you do," she muttered, with a smile, throwing

back her hair. "I appear to have set things off though. Sorry about that."

"It'll likely be awkward for a while anyway, until everybody deals with it," Tiffany noted. "That is not a reason to stay away."

"Nope, but it's a reason to not come back very often," she pointed out. "In a way it's my fault. I should have let him know in the first place."

"I'm surprised you didn't. Why is that?"

"I guess I figured he would just …"

"What? That he would run?" Tiffany asked, with half a laugh.

"I don't know quite what I'm supposed to do."

"What do you mean? You filed for the divorce, right?"

"Yes, and I do think it's the best thing," she explained. "He's a different person now. He's not the person I married."

"No, not at all," Tiffany agreed, not holding back. "He's been through his own hell and back, his own set of recoveries, and I think, in his mind now, his own betrayals. And, if that wasn't enough, then you served him with divorce papers."

She winced. "Yeah, and that just makes me feel as if I did something wrong."

"If you tried to salvage your marriage, and it didn't work, that's not wrong because you tried. That is just life," Tiffany said, giving her a side look. "Yet there's no miracle ending for all this. However, if a part of you thinks you made a hasty decision, then it's up to you to give it some time."

"I don't think I can give it time. Look at how he reacted when he saw me today."

"Sure, but consider what he's also dealing with. Look. I don't know where your relationship's at or how ugly it is," Tiffany admitted, "but I do know that he was talking to his lawyer today, and something pissed him right off."

She looked at her and nodded. "Yeah, I'm not surprised. The attorney I'm working with is a hard-ass."

"And why are you working with that lawyer then? How much could you really have to settle in a legal sense?" Tiffany asked shrewdly. "Do you need a divorce attorney to be a hard-ass? That's pretty rough stuff for a guy who just came back from the military, broken and needing a hand, only to turn around and find out that the hand was to serve divorce papers." Tiffany faced her friend and nodded. "And I get it, not my business," she conceded, "but it's obvious that both of you are hurting."

"Yeah, we're hurting. We both said some things that we probably shouldn't have. Yet I'm not sure we can come back from that."

"There is hope, if you want to," Tiffany pointed out, "and, if you don't want to, then you don't. That's just all there is to it. However, if anything is left of what you once had, maybe you need to take another look."

Keisha laughed. "You make it sound so easy."

"I don't know that it's easy, but I'm really not sure that it's that difficult, not if you really want it," Tiffany reiterated. "I think *difficult* comes in all forms, and there's just not always an easy form. Yet, if you can find a way that won't torment both of you, then maybe it's worth finding a way to talk to him."

"Does it look like he's ready to talk to me?" Keisha quipped.

"No, but then he's got divorce papers on his plate and a

hard-ass attorney on his phone. I don't know what either say, yet I'm pretty sure that's an ending he's not quite ready for."

"Oh, I think he's ready for it. He barely even spoke to me."

"What do you expect him to do?" Tiffany asked. "He hasn't seen you hardly at all. He's recovering from a harsh accident and the surgery and the rehab, then comes home—expecting to see you and to have that life that's held him in good stead all this time. That dream has sustained him through his hospital time, only to find that you're waiting with papers instead."

"He wasn't the same person," she argued.

"None of them are," Tiffany declared immediately. "Absolutely none of them are, but that doesn't mean the person they are now isn't still somebody you want. You just have to figure out if you even know who and what that somebody is and whether it's all worth fighting for." And, with that, she gave her friend a hug and added, "I'm not trying to be philosophical or difficult or anything else."

"Too bad," she muttered, "because you're pretty good at it."

"I know, and I'm sorry," she said, raising both hands. "I found Timber, and I guess I'm in that honeymoon phase, where I want everybody else to be happy. And I know you were happy before with Jaxon. I don't know what happened. I just know that you're not happy now, and neither is he, and surely that says something too." With that she gave her another hug and added, "Drive carefully. The roads are really cut up, so they're on the rough side."

"Yeah, you're not kidding," she agreed. "My truck was bouncing on the way over here."

"Maybe it needs new springs."

"Maybe," she noted, "but, like you, all my money goes into the practice."

"I appreciate you taking your Sunday and coming out to help."

At that, the two women parted, leaving Tiffany to walk up to the front door and stand on the front porch. Timber came out and wrapped an arm around her shoulders.

CHAPTER 5

K EISHA REVERSED, PULLED the big truck around into a circle, then slowly headed down the driveway. Out of the corner of her eye she saw something and almost hit the brakes to stop. Jaxon stood here, out of the way, watching her. On impulse, she lifted a hand and waved at him, not surprised but still disappointed when he didn't wave back.

She thought about him a lot as she returned to town. She probably shouldn't have come without notifying him first, but at least their initial face-to-face meeting after her divorce papers had been served was over. Now if only she had a good excuse or explanation for why she just couldn't handle this new Jaxon. He was definitely no longer the witty man she knew from before—or at least not with her. Maybe he seemed different because she had changed too.

Maybe they were just strangers. They'd gotten married very quickly, and she'd been worried it was a mistake right from the get-go. Tiffany was right in that Keisha hadn't really given him a chance. When he'd come back such a different person, she immediately ran to the safety of what she thought she knew, and somehow that just made her feel even worse than she did when she had first laid eyes on him again.

She'd known he was at the Haven, but seeing him there hadn't brought any recognition. Nothing of the new Jaxon remotely resembled the old him. She felt she was meeting a stranger. It was horrible. She understood that Jaxon wanted to immediately pick up their marriage as if nothing tragic had happened to him, just going back to the way they had been in those few short months before he had been deployed. Yet, for her, she didn't know this Jaxon.

She wasn't bothered about the prosthetic, although she was still surprised that any device would support such a burly man. In fact, she wasn't bothered by any of his physical injuries, even though she didn't have anywhere near the complete info on that. She was, however, more worried about his psychological trauma. She had grown up with a father who had been extremely traumatized by his military years, and Keisha just didn't think she could handle Jaxon's traumas too—or at least that's what she told herself.

Tiffany's voice came in Keisha's head, asking, *So why marry a man who was in the military?*

Keisha sighed. She hadn't been open and honest enough in her own mind to confront whatever was going on in her own thoughts. But now, it all stared her in the face, giving her an opportunity to do something about it, but what?

She'd already filed the divorce papers. She had already broken everybody's heart in this process, including her own. Going back didn't seem to be an option. But was it?

On the way back into town, she couldn't stop thinking about Jaxon and whether she was doing the right thing. Sure, she could halt the process but not before she had the time needed to get to know him again, and maybe that was more of an issue. Yet everything inside her said that time wouldn't help, and, if not time, maybe she was better off just getting the divorce over with. At least that's what she told herself.

As soon as she hit the highway, she picked up speed and

headed back to the clinic. By the time she parked her work truck, switched over to her personal car, she already felt the effects of the long day, and getting home was even harder.

Entering the house, she called out to her sister, "Hey, Kelly. I'm home." Her two rescue dogs, Harley and Homer raced to greet her, their barks and whines and twisting bodies always such a joy to see and experience. Particularly when their joy was at seeing her.

The loud sounds of Kelly's wheelchair being pushed around the house let Keisha know exactly where her sister was and what progress she was making. She smiled as she looked at her younger sister. "How was your day?"

"The usual," she muttered, with that same dismissive wave of her hand. "Not a whole lot I can do."

"I know," Keisha agreed, tamping down her irritation at her sister's constant lack of cheerfulness. Kelly was almost ten years younger, so she didn't have the wisdom of living on her own or of holding a job. She had had their parents stolen from her at a young age. Keisha knew all that and reminded herself of it daily. Still, Kelly had much available to her to make her life a little easier. However, her personality didn't allow for that, didn't make for an easy life for Kelly or for Keisha—or for Jaxon either. In fact, Kelly often sported negative criticism and … just plain nastiness because of the situation she was in now.

She'd been in an ugly car accident a few years back, a car accident where they'd lost their parents. It had been hard on both of them. The real kicker was finding out that Kelly wouldn't walk again. It had torn apart the sisters for the longest time, but they were to the point now where this was the life they had. Keisha had accepted it, but Kelly hadn't.

Keisha smiled at her and asked, "Don't suppose you

started anything for dinner, did you?"

"No, I wasn't feeling very well," she replied immediately.

She nodded. "Yeah, I hear you," she murmured.

"Yeah, … you hear me, but you don't understand me," she snapped.

She looked over at Kelly and sighed. "Look. I'm really tired, and I'm not in the mood."

She glared at her and snapped, "I'm not in the mood either." And, with that, she pushed her wheelchair out of the living room and headed to her first-floor bedroom.

With a sigh, Keisha walked upstairs to her bedroom, where she proceeded to strip out of her dirty clothes and quickly had a shower. She would have to do something about food for the two of them because Kelly sure wouldn't. She had a lot of qualities that were really lovely and helpful, but, when she was in this mood, absolutely nothing was lovely or helpful about her.

And yet Keisha couldn't judge Kelly for her attitude because Keisha wasn't the one sitting in a wheelchair, looking at the ruins of her life. At one point in time, Kelly had planned on being a fashion designer and had had remarkable success with some of her early designs, but the accident had changed all that. She could potentially still go back to that, but she no longer had the strength to get through most of her days, and the evenings were even rougher.

Knowing that it was even harder on her sister than on her, Keisha bit down on her frustration, quickly dressed in yoga pants and a T-shirt, then headed downstairs to the kitchen to start dinner. The dogs followed her into the kitchen looking for their own dinners, particularly as she could see their dog bowls were completely empty. After feeding them, she called out, "What do you want for food?"

"I don't care," Kelly snapped, and then she groaned. "Sorry, Keish. … I'm not trying to be a bitch."

"No, I get it. You're having a rough day," she replied.

"Yeah, well, … seems as if I'm only having rough days these days."

Keisha didn't say anything to that. What could she say? Her sister had also refused to go back to the doctors' appointments, whether therapist or shrink or her medical doctors, saying they were useless.

And should she return? Keisha wondered. All the docs wanted to do was poke and prod and ask her questions that she didn't have any answers for. And that might be fair enough, yet, if no answers were there to be found, then why continue this useless process? But if any new medicine, new technology, new anything could help Kelly, then they needed that opportunity to put it to good use. Keisha wanted Kelly to get the help she needed. Not that her sister ever saw it that way.

Looking in the fridge, Keisha decided on pasta, and, with the water on boil, she ended up making a simple carbonara.

By the time Kelly was back in the kitchen, sniffing the aroma, she muttered, "Not pasta again."

Keisha froze and frowned at Kelly. "Yeah, pasta again. I'm tired, Kel. It's been a long day at the clinic. How about just a *thank you* for having cooked anything?"

Her sister rolled her eyes at her. "You always make it sound as if I'm such a trial."

"Sometimes you are. … I put in a long day too."

"Sure, driving around, checking on llamas," she said enviously.

"Yeah, llamas that were tired, hot, cranky, terrified, and

needed to be shorn, even though it wasn't exactly something I was thinking I would help with today," she shared, as she rolled her shoulders, realizing that she hadn't used these muscles in a very long time.

"And, of course, you probably saw your … *husband*," Kelly muttered in a mocking tone, chewing on her words.

Keisha sighed at that. Kelly had never gotten along well with Jaxon, and Jaxon had very little tolerance for her either. "Yes, Jaxon was there," she stated, hiding her face. "And, no, I didn't really talk to him."

"How did he look?"

After a moment of thinking about it, she shared, "Fit, more physically fit than I remember him being. … He looked good. He wasn't very happy to see me though."

"Why would he be?" Kelly asked, followed by a laugh. "You made a decision that he didn't like."

She winced at that and nodded. "Potentially that was it, and honestly, I don't know that I made the right decision either." The words popped out before she had a chance to pull them back.

Kelly stared at her. "You're not thinking about going back after all that, are you?"

"After all what?" she asked, turning to look at her sister. "I'm not even sure how I came around to that decision in the first place."

Kelly laughed. "Of course you are," she declared, still snickering. "Just the fact that you see him once and are all over him again is just unbelievable."

"Maybe, and maybe I just don't know what I want."

"Of course you don't know what you want," Kelly stated, her eyes squinting. "Yet you were pretty quick to ditch him when he got home, weren't you?"

She stared at her sister. "That's not fair."

"Sure, it's fair," she argued, with a shrug. "I'm sitting here, watching you go to pieces, trying to help you make all the right decisions, and yet … you see him once, and there you are, all over him again."

"No, that's not true," Keisha countered, staring at Kelly. "I don't remember how that divorce decision came about in the first place. I just remember thinking that he was a completely different person and that I didn't know him anymore."

"That's exactly how you get to those kinds of decisions," Kelly noted, frowning at her. "You realize that the person you married isn't the same person anymore."

"Maybe not," Keisha muttered. "Anyway, it doesn't matter, and he was looking fine today."

"*Looking fine*," Kelly repeated, then shook her head. "Jesus Christ, if you turn around and go backward again on this whole thing …"

"I'm not going backward. There is no backward to even go." She stared at Kelly, shook her head, and muttered, "Jesus Christ."

"What?"

"Never mind." Keisha quickly served dinner, giving her sister a plate and then sat down to eat herself.

Kelly stared at the food on the plate and immediately said, "I'm not hungry." And she wheeled herself away.

Realizing that Kelly's issue was all because of the talk about Jaxon, Keisha called out, "I'm not going back on my word."

"Not yet but you will. He'll snap his fingers, and, just like that, you'll be gone again," Kelly spat, tears in her eyes as she stopped at the doorway. "But that's okay too. You go off and do your thing." With that, she turned and wheeled as fast as she could wheel herself down the hallway to her bedroom.

Keisha shook her head. It always ended up this way. Conversations about her and Jaxon ended with Kelly in tears that would take days to calm her down. And, in that moment, Keisha realized that one of the biggest reasons why she had started the whole separation with her husband was because of Kelly.

It wasn't even so much … Then she stopped and whispered to herself, "Now stop it. You can't blame your sister for this. You're the one going through the whole *you don't know who he is anymore* issue."

In all fairness, Kelly had been pretty big on making Keisha see who and what she was, what she was looking for now. So, she couldn't blame her sister for putting herself in this spot. Still, Keisha also didn't understand why seeing him today had changed something in her, and yet it had.

Confused, frustrated, and angry, Keisha went out for a walk, taking Harley and Homer. Both Heinz fifty-seven mixes of medium build somewhat resembling black labs. But they were company for each other. She should have taken them to The Haven today. They'd have loved it, but she'd left from the clinic early to collect the llamas and deliver them so hadn't thought far enough ahead to take the dogs. She needed to do more trips like that with them. They were pets that she didn't get much of a chance to be with because she was always at the clinic, always working, always doing something, and of course, the *always doing something* part was that she was trying to redo the mess her life was in.

She'd married quickly, and Kelly had disapproved horribly. Jaxon and Kelly did not have a great relationship between them. He'd never had a whole lot of patience for Kelly, and Kelly had left no doubt about her intolerance for him. Then he'd been deployed, and he was gone. The timing had been good because Keisha couldn't handle the bickering between Jaxon and Kelly anymore. So, with him on assignment, Keisha and Kelly had settled into a more pleasant routine. Then, all of a sudden, he returned, but he was damaged, injured, and Keisha just hadn't known how to handle it.

They'd been apart just long enough that she felt single again and had loved the peace and quiet of being home with one less person to consider. Although she had missed him terribly, she hadn't missed the problems with Jaxon and her sister, to the point that Keisha wondered if she had made the wrong choice in marrying Jaxon.

Kelly had been quick to point out all the things that were wrong with him, and Keisha had listened. Whether that was right or wrong, she didn't know, and now she wondered how much she had just wanted that peace and quiet and how unfair that was to him.

Tears in her eyes, she headed back home. When her cell phone rang, she answered it almost absentmindedly.

"So, did you go see him?" asked the computerized voice on the other end, followed by mocking laughter.

Not knowing who was calling her, Keisha disconnected.

But she recognized this cruel taunting nonetheless because Keisha had been tormented online to the point that she had stopped using any social media accounts—all because this one person kept bugging her about her partner, about what a waste of space he was. Broken, useless, somebody this particular person didn't want to be seen with.

So, Keisha had deactivated every online SM account she

had, not knowing how this person had even gotten a hold of her, and yet they had. Then, out of the blue, they got her phone number. It had driven Keisha batty, but she hadn't told anybody, and it shouldn't have played any part in her decision to divorce Jaxon. Yet always lingering on the edge of her subconscious was the idea that all these problems would go away if she divorced him.

Again, not fair to him and not fair to the ache in her heart either. Yet somehow, somewhere along the line, life had seemed so much easier *before*.

With a heavy sigh, she walked back up to the house and realized her sister had locked the door while she was out, so Keisha was forced to call her.

When Kelly finally opened the door, she glared at her. "Like I need more exercise in a day," she snapped.

"I'm sorry, but I didn't realize you were locking up."

"I didn't lock up," she declared, staring at her. "That was you." And, with that, she turned in a huff and headed back to her bedroom.

Keisha wasn't sure whether she had or hadn't, but had been tired enough that maybe she had made such a mistake. She felt foolish and worn out and quickly headed to bed. As soon as she got there, she couldn't sleep. Every thought, every deed, every act, every insecurity she had just piled on to the point that she didn't even know what she was doing anymore.

Then, just when she was almost asleep, the phone call came again.

Private Number.

These crank calls never came with a number. She immediately answered and asked, "How did you get this number?"

The mechanical voice laughed, and then it disconnected.

Shaky, worried, sad, and confused, Keisha finally fell into a deep but fitful sleep.

She woke up the next morning, exhausted and worn out, wondering what the hell she was doing with her life. Confused and tired, she collapsed back again, this time finding a way to sleep a little bit longer and, to a certain extent, a little bit better.

CHAPTER 6

"**W**HAT'S WITH THE phone calls?" Timber asked, as Jaxon looked at the screen on his phone in disgust, then pocketed it again.

"I don't know. I'm getting hassled by somebody. It's been going on for a while. I just don't know who it is."

"Obviously that is disconcerting."

"If I had the money to figure it out, I would do something about it," Jaxon noted, with a shrug. "Sometimes you get people who just want to play around and to mess up your world, and I don't have time to fix it."

"No, of course not, but if there's anything we can do …"

He smirked. "Do you have anybody who can handle this techie stuff?"

"Yeah, I do," Timber said, nodding at him, "at least to a certain extent." He turned to Tommy, who was serving up a plate of food. Tommy was the most tech savvy of the military personnel at the Haven just now. He had come since Timber got started building on the property. Tommy helped them set up the medical clinic, and, even now, he did as much as he could with the chores and whatever else was needed. "Tommy, what about that buddy of yours?"

"Yeah, that's Gregory." He looked to Jaxon and shrugged. "He is a digital PI. He's busy, but I know he won't mind taking a look to see what the problem is." He quickly contacted him and told him about the situation. Tommy laughed at whatever Gregory had said on the other end. "No, that's another one. That one was Burke."

"Oh, this is the guy who helped Burke?" Jaxon asked, turning to Timber.

He nodded. "Yeah, Gregory helped resolve the credit card fraud issues and some other online trouble that Burke had."

Just then Tommy came over, his phone in hand, laughing, still talking to Gregory. "Apparently these guys collect trouble." Then he passed over his phone.

With the phone now in his possession, Jaxon talked to Tommy's friend and explained what the problem was.

"It's probably just a phishing con or something," Gregory suggested. "Give me your number."

Providing the number, Jaxon heard clicking on the other end.

"And what about the number of the caller?"

"It just comes up as a Private Number."

"Great, so either it's a burner phone or a computer app, which would imply a little bit more exuberance or interest in ruining your life. Anybody in this world hate you?"

"My soon-to-be ex-wife," he replied. "She started divorce proceedings."

"That might do it. Does she have a partner?"

His heart clenched at that. "I honestly don't have a clue."

Gregory went silent for a moment, then added, "Okay, leave it with me for a few days, and I'll see what I can come up with." And, with that, Gregory disconnected.

Jaxon returned the phone to Tommy. "Gregory will get back to me."

"Yeah, he'll run through everything he can and try to find whatever there is, and either something will be there or not." Tommy sighed. "It's never the answer we quite expect or want, yet he's often right."

"That's both good and depressing."

"Yeah, he would say the same thing," Tommy agreed, with a wry smile. "He's a good guy."

"What will I owe him for this?"

"Depends on what he finds, sometimes nothing," he replied, with a shrug. "Sometimes he just thinks it's a shit deal, and people are people, and he doesn't want to take payment for stopping these kinds of problems, but I can't guarantee that. Everybody's got to eat."

"Right, and that's fine too."

"You good for money?" Tommy asked.

"Yeah, if I have anything left after the divorce," Jaxon said, with a groan, "that'll be something to pay him with."

"She's got a vet clinic, so she should be the one who's paying you," teased one of the men. A few *Hell yeah* comments could be heard.

Jaxon looked around and frowned. "I don't think I could live with that."

"Maybe not, but, depending on how much of your pension and everything else she's planning on taking, you're not likely to end up with anything to live on."

"Which would really suck," he muttered.

"Yeah, you're not kidding. It all depends on who she is as a person."

"Generally indecisive," he muttered. "That's probably one of the biggest things I would say, and she's got a sister who she's basically looking after."

"Why is that?"

He explained about the car accident, and they all winced.

One said, "You understand that perfectly well."

"I do now," Jaxon admitted, "but back then? I had very little tolerance for her, so I was definitely part of the problem."

"What was the rub?"

"She's one of those people who just sits there, complaining about her lot in life, and expects to be waited on. I didn't have much patience for it." He sighed, as he looked down at his own rebuilt body. "Maybe I would feel differently about Kelly now."

"Maybe your wife couldn't handle the strife again," Roman suggested.

"Maybe, but it would have been nice if she'd given us the chance to figure out if we even had a problem before starting divorce proceedings."

"Sometimes it happens that way," Big Toby announced from the doorway.

"I came back, and my wife was already long gone," Roman shared, sorrow still in his tone. "There was no, *Hi, welcome back* or anything else. Nobody was home, and the divorce papers were waiting on the counter, which is the last thing we need while we're overseas or coming back from that assignment."

Jaxon winced at that and nodded. "Sorry about that."

"Stop feeling sorry for yourself, Roman," Dwight barked.

"I'm not," Roman declared. "It's been quite a few years now, so whatever, but it still left a bad taste. We can't blame anybody for being that person, but ..."

Just then Jaxon's phone rang again. He stared down at it and swore.

Timber held out his hand, looked at the Caller ID, and asked, "Just says Private Number, *huh?*"

"Yeah, Private Number, computerized voice, no clue what all this harassment and taunting is all about. If I answer it, there'll be a mocking laugh."

"Answer it," Timber said, "and put it on Speaker."

He immediately answered it and that same mocking laugh that he'd come to hate filled the air.

Everybody just stared at it. "That's like the Chucky doll nightmare horror stuff," Roman noted, staring at it. "God, that's creepy."

"Right, and not a whole lot I can do about it."

"That one is definitely weird."

Timber stared down at the phone and asked, "How often are you getting these calls?"

"Lately, it's been more," he shared. "Overseas, I used to get it every once in a while, but then it was more … I don't know how to describe it, but it was off and on. Now that I'm back, they're just out there, constantly pushing buttons."

He nodded. "That sucks."

"Yeah, it pretty much does," Jaxon agreed, with a shrug, and went back to eating his breakfast. "What's on top of the list for today?"

Timber glared up at the whiteboard that had become the nemesis for everybody here. "Shirley has the board nicely refilled," Timber muttered, turning his glare on the young woman sitting on the other side of the kitchen table.

Shirley was an absolute dream project manager. She just let Timber rant and rave, and, if through the course of the conversation she heard anything else useful, she would get up and add it to the board while he watched, which usually sent him into another tailspin.

She smiled at him. "You're doing fine, Timber," she called out. "Pretty soon you'll have some of this stuff beaten."

He rolled his eyes at that and groaned. "Ya think?"

"Yep, I think," she confirmed, with that smile still in place. "It will be a while yet, but the longer you guys just sit here and commiserate, the longer it will be."

With exaggerated sighs and varied complaints, several of the men got up, but their plates were well and truly empty, and Shirley knew it. They joked and laughed, mostly over anything else, but it was still a great working environment.

The progress she spoke of was something Timber really hoped to accomplish for himself and for the Haven, but he also knew she probably had volumes of items to add to the whiteboards as soon as some space was cleared. That depressing thought was interrupted by the ringing of a phone, and he turned his attention back to Jaxon.

CHAPTER 7

JAXON SIGHED AS he answered it, not recognizing the number. "Hello?" He then froze. "Keisha, what's the matter?"

"It's Kelly," she muttered, her voice choked with tears.

"What about her?" He turned to Timber and swore. "What's wrong with Kelly? ... She's had another incident?" he repeated, trying to hear through Keisha's tears and sobbing. "Where are you?"

Everyone focused on him, as he repeated back, "Okay, so you're at the hospital now? Do you want me to call somebody?" he asked, then realized she'd called him because, chances were, she had nobody else. He swore at that.

Immediately Timber said, "Go." When Jaxon frowned, Timber shook his head. "Go on. We all need help when we need help."

He sighed and spoke to Keisha. "I'm heading into town, so I'll come by the hospital, okay? I'm on my way." Hearing her sobs on the other end, he finally managed to get her to understand that he was coming to see her. With that done, he disconnected, then turned and glared at Timber. "Why am I seeing her?"

"First, she's hurting. Second, she called you, which means she doesn't have anybody else. Third, you're already trying to figure out how to stop her from this whole divorce thing, so this is a really good way for you guys to sit down and talk."

"Yeah? Who said I wanted to talk?" he muttered.

"Doesn't matter if you want to or not," Timber noted in a cheerful booming tone. "It's a good time to talk regardless." And, with that, he got up.

Shirley grabbed Timber by the arm. "Perfect timing for us too," she shared. "I was looking for a meeting with you."

"Oh, no, no, no," he muttered, trying to jerk his arm free. "I've got work to do."

"Yep, you sure do," she declared, sweetness in her tone. "We have to go over the clinic list. Some things need your attention there."

"What? Did Tiffany put you up to that?" he asked.

"No, but I noticed the intakes of the llamas and alpacas yesterday," she explained. "So, we definitely need to go over a few things."

"Fine, fine, fine." He groaned. "You know there's no money for all this, right?" he asked, with a wave of his hand at the board.

She nodded at him. "There wasn't any money to begin with either, as far as I understood, so it doesn't really matter to me. These projects are all on the in-progress list, just so we can set up priorities and make them happen." He rolled his eyes, and she laughed. "Grab another coffee and let's go."

In a surprise move—since Timber was generally someone who nobody ordered around—he grabbed a second cup of coffee and then stepped up to the whiteboards, where they immediately huddled together in a deep discussion.

Jaxon stared down at the half-eaten food on the plate in front of him.

Toby showed up with a to-go cup in his hand. "You better get going to the hospital." When Jaxon responded with a glare, Toby nodded. "You and I both know you need to go," he stated. "And, if you're honest, we both know you want to. Now, here's some coffee for the road."

And, with that, the table was more or less moved out from under him, and he was standing here, holding a to-go cup. Jaxon sighed, then asked, "Do you need anything from town?"

Toby pondered that and frowned. "I'll let you know. Call me before you come back."

"Will do," Jaxon muttered, then headed out to his vehicle.

CHAPTER 8

KEISHA WASN'T EVEN sure why she'd called Jaxon. She had absolutely no reason to, and yet he was the first and only person she could think of to call. As she sat here in the waiting room outside the ER, nervously waiting on the doctor, she looked up, responding to that inner sense of knowing that Jaxon was here. He walked toward her, a cup of coffee in his hand. She looked at the coffee and sighed. "At least you got a cup."

"I did. Do you want some of it?" He held out the cup.

She smiled, then nodded. "Yeah, we always took it the same way, didn't we?"

"Still do," he muttered, "unless you've changed."

"Apparently we've both changed," she noted, as she took a sip of coffee and realized it was a tad on the hot side still, but, other than that, it was perfect. She had several more sips before she handed it back. "I'm surprised you came," she confessed, surprising herself at her comment too.

"I'm surprised you called."

She winced. "So am I."

He looked at her steadily. "What happened to Kelly?"

"I don't know. I found her on the floor, and she was crying like … she fell."

He nodded. "Has that happened very often?"

"No, not very often and, usually when it does happen,

it's a sign of seizures or something. I didn't even realize when I called you what I was doing," she admitted. "So, if you need to leave, I understand."

He stared at her steadily. "You called. I said I would come. I'm here," he declared. "Now we figure out what's going on with Kelly."

"She won't like you being here."

"No, she probably won't," he agreed, "but that doesn't mean that leaving is the right thing to do."

She looked over at him and smiled. "It's always about the right thing with you, isn't it?"

"No, but it's often not that hard to determine what's right and what's wrong," he pointed out. "Right now, staying here and seeing what the doctor says is the right thing."

She sat back, and he passed her the coffee again. She immediately accepted it, wishing the doctor would show up. When the double doors to the ER rooms opened, and he stepped through a few minutes later, he looked for her immediately and then smiled. "Not sure exactly what happened," he shared, with a nod. "She's fallen obviously, but appears to be doing okay."

Keisha felt the relief washing through her. "Thank God for that." She scrubbed her face. "When I found her on the floor, she was barely moving, hardly talking, not fully conscious. I didn't know what she was saying. I didn't know if she was awake or asleep," she muttered.

"No drugs were in her system, so I don't know if she's been taking her pain meds or not. It also seems that some of her other medications haven't been taken on a regular basis. Her bowels are compacted."

She winced at that and shared, "I haven't been keeping

close tabs on her these last few days. I've been pretty busy."

"She's an adult, and she's perfectly capable of looking after herself," the doc stated.

"Sure, but, for everybody in life," she pointed out, "it's easier when you're not alone."

"Oh, that I understand," he agreed, with a beaming smile. "I just don't want you blaming yourself if you weren't there to confirm whether she took her meds as she was supposed to."

"Right, well, … let's hope that she'll be okay. May I take her home?"

"In a little bit. We'll do a couple checks on her just to confirm everything is as it's supposed to be," he replied. "I'm not worried about her, but she hasn't kept her appointments in the last year, which is unfortunate, but we do tend to see that avoidance sometimes with patients who are struggling a little bit … mentally."

"Mentally?" she repeated, frowning at him. "Are you thinking she's depressed?"

"I don't know if it's more depression or just low energy levels or a lack of self-care. … We tend to see these symptoms sometimes," he explained carefully, "when their personal care drops."

"Ah." Keisha nodded. "I guess that's possible. She's been a little upset lately."

"Anything in particular?"

"No, not really," she said, with a smile. "Just upset at … where she's at in life."

"Ah, well, counseling is probably a really good answer for that."

"She stopped going a while back," she shared, "and I've been trying to get her to return, but, so far, she's been resisting my efforts."

He didn't say anything immediately, but he nodded. "We see that too," he added. "Maybe suggest art therapy or even bring her to your clinic to hold a dog or a cat. That helps so many people."

Keisha sighed. "She doesn't want to leave the house and acts so rudely when I force her out that I don't care to try anymore."

The doctor gave her a knowing smile and nodded. "Give us a little bit of time to talk with her, to see where she's at health-wise. She'll be home today for sure, but maybe go have breakfast or something. Then you and your husband can come back a little bit later."

She sighed. "Thank you. May I see her now?"

"No, not at the moment," he stated. "Just give us a little time to treat her and to make some assessments. Then you can come back and see her afterward." She frowned and he smiled. "She's fine—honestly."

"I know, but I want to see her."

"You can absolutely see her," he replied, then hesitated. "I didn't want to have to tell you, but she doesn't want to see you right now."

She stared at him. "I see. … Well, that's pretty clear."

"No, it's not clear at all," he countered, with a thoughtful nod. "I'm not sure what's bringing that on, but I'll talk to her. Give me a chance to spend some time with her while she's here. I think I may bring in a specialist as well."

She frowned at him and asked, "You mean, a psychologist?"

"Yes, somebody who can see if she's in an okay state of mind."

And, on that note, she looked at Jaxon.

He nodded. "Come on. Let's go get some coffee and some food." Then he led her outside.

She stared at the parking lot. "Why do you think she doesn't want to see me?"

"It depends," Jaxon suggested. "If she fell, she may feel bad because it's a reminder that she can't look after herself. You may have reacted to this fall by reaming her out because she wasn't looking after herself, and she wanted to avoid all that. You and I both know there could be a multitude of answers to that question."

She groaned, rotated her shoulders slightly, and replied, "You're right. That sounds very much like her."

"She's never …"

"She's never what?" she asked, with a challenging tone.

"I would say, she has never appeared to be an easy patient."

She stared at him and realized he was trying to couch his words and to not upset her. She really had no business being upset, not when he's the one who came at her request. "You're right. She's not been easy, but then her life isn't particularly easy either."

"Of course not," he agreed, "and I didn't mean any insult."

"I'm just supersensitive," she shared, with a wave of her hand.

He pointed out to the parking lot. "Come on. We'll take my truck. You got any favorite breakfast spots?"

"There's the one," she began, turning to him.

He nodded, heading to a spot they had been to many times.

As they pulled up to the front of the restaurant, she sighed. "This does feel like old times."

He parked and nodded. "Let's go."

She hopped out on her side, and, as they walked inside the restaurant, she realized he had reached out a hand, and she had accepted it. They still held hands as they walked into the restaurant. She stared down at their intertwined hands as they followed the waitress. "How did we fall back into this?" she whispered.

"I don't know," he said, with a shrug, "and I hate to tell you, but it feels kind of right."

She wasn't sure what to say to that. As they took a seat, he dropped her hand and waited for her to sit, with that same old Southern charm that came so easily to him. It had always been a boon in the relationship because it always made her feel as if he cared. And that was the thing. He did care. He had always cared. As she slipped into her spot, she looked over at him. "Thank you for coming."

"Of course," he said.

"I didn't think you would."

"I wasn't sure I would either. We were just setting up the work for the day," he shared, with a smile, "and my boss was like, 'Nope, get going.' So, given a free pass to leave, … here I am."

"But he's not really your boss, is he?"

"If you're asking if I'm getting paid, the answer is no. I'm not getting paid. If you're asking if he's leading the team, and since we're all there to help and to be part of the team," he explained, "then yes. … He's the boss, and, when you're on a team, you follow the boss and the team."

She waited for the waitress to leave after delivering their coffee. As Keisha picked up her cup, she asked, "That's something that would fit right along the line for you, isn't it?"

"Meaning?" he asked curiously.

"Just that you're used to working as part of a team."

"I am," he confirmed. "It's a lot like the military and how we lived."

"Right, so being part of a team right now is something that would make you feel comfortable."

"Yeah," he agreed. "It is comforting to know where you stand with people and to know that they have your back."

She immediately flushed. "I guess I had that coming."

"I didn't mean it in that way," he said, "but you asked, and I was just trying to explain how having a team be there for me is huge."

She didn't say anything for a long moment, and then finally she nodded. "I never really had much of that."

"No, it doesn't seem like you have," he acknowledged, as he pondered it. "At least from what I know of your life, that's not something you've really been exposed to. In a way, it's too bad because it's been huge for me. It's amazing to know that I have people there for me, no matter what."

Keisha nodded. He was right. That would be nice. But she'd been alone with Kelly for a long time, and Keisha looked after Kelly, but Keisha couldn't imagine Kelly looking after her if their situations had been reversed. Keisha didn't say anything for a long moment and finally nodded again. "Not something I really recognize."

The waitress returned with menus, and, as they sat here, considering their food options, she looked over at him and asked, "Is there anything that you want here?"

"I'll have the usual," he replied. "I had a little breakfast with the team, but I can always eat more."

She snorted at that. "It seems as if there was never a time that you couldn't eat more."

"Nope, lots of calories get burned up, so putting more calories to good use never seems to be a bad idea," he noted, with a smile.

They quickly placed their orders, and, as they waited for their meals to come, she looked over at him. "I'm sorry yesterday was so awkward."

"The good news is, today isn't as awkward," he pointed out immediately.

She gave a half laugh and then nodded. "Isn't that the truth?"

"It's also not what I expected."

"It's not what I expected either."

His phone rang just then, and he groaned as he stared down at the number.

"Problems?" she asked.

"I've been getting a lot of spam calls recently," he shared, shaking his head. "I'm not sure who is doing it, but I've been targeted by somebody."

She frowned at that. "And it always says, Private Number?"

"Yeah, did you see it?"

"No," she replied, "but I've been in a similar situation." He frowned at her, and she nodded. "I'm not really sure what it's all about, but it's been disquieting to have it happen."

"Of course," he agreed. "Any idea who it is?"

"No."

"Did they ask for anything?"

"No, just this weird laughter."

"Same here," he said, staring at her. "It's just a really weird laugh, computer-generated or whatever, that makes no sense."

She nodded. "Yeah, that's exactly what I've been getting."

"Why would they target both of us?"

"I don't know," she admitted, nodding. "However, I didn't know they were targeting you, so who's to say that they're targeting us? You're assuming it's the same person."

"You're right," he stated, taking a deep breath. "Although it's odd that the two of us would have different cyberstalkers."

"This was happening before," she shared. "I used to have social media accounts, and I shut them all down. For a while, it was really disturbing to go online and to find people posting really awful things on my accounts."

He stared at her. "You never mentioned it."

"It happened just after you were deployed," she added, staring off in the distance and thinking about it. "I never really clued in on what was going on until quite a while afterward. It seemed to stop for a while. Then it just picked up and came back, meaner than ever." She shrugged. "And who knows? … I don't know what they're after, or what their story is, but I didn't want to give them the satisfaction of knowing they were upsetting me."

"Did you ever tell anybody?"

"No," she replied. "I didn't tell anybody, including Kelly. I didn't want her to worry."

"Why not?"

"She's always told me not to hand out any information on the internet, and, of course, I must have somewhere along the line," she concluded. "It's weird because I didn't think I had, but …"

"Right, and, even if you did, it doesn't mean we should be targeted like that," he pointed out.

"No, but it doesn't stop some people."

Their meals came just then, and they talked while they were eating, having completely different conversations. When he finally came up for air, she was smiling at him, sitting back with a second cup of coffee. "I forgot how you ate."

He nodded. "I'm still healing, still building back muscle."

Her smile fell away, and she frowned. "You never did tell me a whole lot about what was going on in that rehab center."

"If you would have showed up, I could have shown you."

She winced. "If I wasn't still getting the clinic set up, I might have been able to," she murmured.

"I understood that," he noted, with a shrug. "I was really looking forward to coming back and helping you."

"Helping me?" she repeated.

"Yeah, helping you." He rolled his eyes as he saw her jerk in response. "I don't know in what capacity, but I was really proud of you and was looking forward to being part of this new life for you." She just stared at him as he spoke. "And then you showed up at the Haven to help with rescued llamas of all things."

"Ah." She nodded, with a sigh. "What else will you do when animals are in need?"

"That's exactly how Timber feels," Jaxon pointed out. "By the time he's done, he'll have room for hundreds of animals on that place."

"I've been hearing about it from Tiffany. She's overwhelmed with joy at what he's creating out there."

"She's also been a huge help in defining how things

should be set up," he noted, with a smile. "It's not necessarily the most economical or affordable input, but she's trying to lay things out in a way that makes sense."

She smiled. "That's Tiffany for you. She's always got an idea, always got something going, always busy."

"Just like Timber," he said, with a laugh. "The two of them are well matched."

"She seems really happy," Keisha noted. "I think they both are."

He looked over at her with a wry smile. "See? Not everybody is unhappy being together." She flushed at that. "You never did really tell me why you want a divorce."

"I'm not sure I could tell you even now." When he stared at her in surprise, she nodded. "I don't even know what to say, except that it feels as if we're two different people."

"You're right. We are two different people," he confirmed, "but that doesn't mean we're two different people who can't make a life together." When she tilted her head, he smiled. "We didn't even give ourselves a chance to get to know each other again."

"Maybe," she murmured, "it just seemed as if everything was moving so fast when you came home, and I just couldn't adjust to you and my sister fighting. It just—"

He nodded. "And, for that, I owe you my apologies," he acknowledged. "I didn't handle her very well when I got back. She was so insulting that it was hard to not tell her to get her ass out of the house and to do something with her life."

"She was insulting?" she asked, staring at him.

"Yeah, she was insulting, and you were okay with it."

"No, I was never okay with it," she declared, leaning

forward, "but I don't remember if I ever heard her … insulting you. To me, it seemed as if you had no patience with her, and, every time I turned around, she was in tears."

"That could be," he said. "She was in tears a lot."

Keisha winced at that. "You're right. She was in tears a lot, but I don't think that's necessarily anything I can judge her for."

"You shouldn't judge her anyway," he stated, with a smile. "She's living a life that is hard for anybody to understand."

"And yet yours isn't a whole lot better."

"Oh, mine is way better," he declared, staring at her. "However, just because I'm not in a wheelchair doesn't mean I don't know what she's going on about. I do know lots of people in wheelchairs, but we're not here to talk about her."

"Essentially we are," Keisha clarified, with a wry look on her face. "That's what brought us in here."

He frowned at that and then nodded. "I guess you're right about that. Is she doing anything, like taking any classes or—"

"No, nothing. She's had a rough couple months."

"Yeah, a *rough couple months* seems to be the status quo for all of us right now."

She looked at him and winced. "I didn't mean it that way."

He looked over at her, shrugged, and didn't say any more.

In that moment, she realized just how much she'd hurt him. She didn't know what to say, and, when her phone rang, it was the hospital saying she could come and get her sister. She looked over at him. "She's ready to be picked up. Would you mind dropping me off at the hospital?"

"Nope, that's fine," he replied, getting up. As they got to the hospital, he added, "I won't come in. It would likely just upset Kelly even more."

Keisha frowned and then acknowledged that. "You're right. It probably would. Listen. I really appreciate that you came when I called." As she stepped out of his vehicle, she turned to him and added, "Maybe we should go for coffee again one day."

CHAPTER 9

T HE NEXT MORNING, Keisha got up, headed to the
clinic, looking at a long full day, since every day seemed
to be that way. She even ran home at noon to check on
Kelly, who sent her away, almost angry that she felt the need
to come home and check on her baby sister.

With a sigh, Keisha headed back out again, wondering
how to make life a little easier on her sister. It was something
she wanted to talk to Kelly about, but her sister was so
resistant to everything right now—particularly after this
latest fall—that Keisha really wasn't sure what to do. All day
she kept it in the back of her mind, and she also couldn't
stop thinking about Jaxon. She hadn't expected to reach out
to him, but neither had she expected him to reach back. But
he did and had been there for her in every way.

She groaned, wondering what the hell she was doing
with her life by filing for a divorce. Why she had even gone
in that direction? Yet she couldn't imagine any other option.
If she'd asked him for a break, or a chance to slowly get used
to having him home again, would that have gone over well?
Not likely.

As far as he was concerned, this was his house too. The
fact that he'd come back home from rehab, and she hadn't
even given him that space to land, also revealed an awful lot
about her, and she didn't like any of it.

Toward the end of the workday, when her vet tech asked her if she was okay, Keisha looked up at her, sighed, and said, "Yeah, just, you know, personal problems."

"Those are the devil for all of us," she agreed. "If there's anything I can do to help somehow, let me know." And, with that, her tech locked up and headed home for the day.

Keisha looked around and realized she'd gone through the entire day but had little recollection of the patients and clients she had seen, and that wasn't a good thing at all. It was also very typical when she got caught up in all the problems with Kelly—and now with Jaxon.

She called her sister and asked if she wanted Keisha to pick up something for dinner because she was too tired to cook. Kelly barely answered, giving her a monosyllabic reply. The entirety of the exchange included, "No, nothing. I don't want to eat."

And that wasn't the right thing either, so, unsure what to do, Keisha picked up groceries anyway, knowing she would have to cook instead of just picking up something to-go that would make her life easier. Yet, if she didn't get her sister to eat, things would go downhill again.

Once she was home, she unloaded the car and headed inside to find her sister in the living room, reading. She barely even looked up. Keisha frowned, headed to the kitchen, then quickly unloaded the groceries. She put on water for pasta and brought out veggies and some really nice Italian sausage she had picked up.

With the meal cooking and feeling some of the fatigue wearing off, she once again picked up the pieces of what was masquerading as her life right now and headed into the living room, adding a smile as she announced, "Dinner is almost ready."

"I'm not hungry," Kelly muttered in a sour tone.

"Maybe not, but you also need to eat, Kel."

"Or what?" she snapped glaring.

"Or else you'll end up in the hospital again, and I know how much you love that," Keisha pointed out in a calm tone, before returning to the kitchen.

She served up dinner, hoping Kelly would get out of her sour mood, but it wasn't to be. Keisha went ahead and sat down to eat, but Kelly still refused to come into the kitchen. Keisha sat here after she'd finished her meal, morosely wondering what avenue she had for helping her sister, yet trying to get her own life back. It would be nice to think a better life was out there for her and Kelly, but Keisha had no idea how to push Kelly, without pushing too far.

Kelly slowly made her way into the kitchen, while Keisha still sat here, hugging a cup of tea. Kelly frowned at Keisha. "What's the matter with you?" she asked.

She shrugged. "I'm tired. It's been a long day. There's pasta if you want it. If not, I'll take it for lunch tomorrow."

"I thought you were buying your lunches out," she remarked in a mocking tone.

"No. That's not in the budget." She frowned at Kelly, trying hard to suppress her anger. "Look. I get it. You don't like your life. You don't like a whole lot about things these days," Keisha pointed out, "but you sure aren't making it easy on me either. There is food if you want it. If not, don't eat. I don't care." Immediately horrified at herself for having said that, Keisha got up and walked out. She headed upstairs to the shower, but it still didn't wash away the guilt from telling off her sister. Keisha probably needed to do more of it, but she didn't have to do it in a mean way. Still, that was hard to do when you were angry.

And why was Keisha angry? Maybe because her entire life was a mess right now, and she didn't have a clue how to fix it. She was also damn confused after having spent time today with Jaxon. The same damn attraction was there, even if she hadn't acknowledged it. She wanted to acknowledge it, and there was no reason why it shouldn't be there. There was nothing wrong with the way she felt.

They were still husband and wife, and they had had a robust relationship prior to his deployment, but then he got injured and eventually came home. So, it's not as if those feelings shouldn't be here, but she was the one who had started the divorce proceedings, and she was wondering how much of it was because she'd been so overwhelmed with his injuries, same as she already felt overwhelmed by Kelly's injuries.

When he had returned, his interactions with Kelly had been brutal, and Keisha had made no effort to understand him or Kelly at all. Keisha had been stuck between a rock and a hard place, with nowhere to go at all. This was Keisha's family home, left to her with the passing of her parents as the eldest child, and Keisha's sister was living here too, yet not thriving at all. It wasn't a good place for Kelly, as far as Keisha could tell, but she knew that any suggestion that Kelly should move out to a special home and should move on with others like her would be met with Kelly's incredible anger and hurt, not to mention a sense of betrayal. Keisha just didn't know what to do.

Her hand automatically reached for her phone to call her own therapist. Then she slowly put her cell down again. It's not that she shouldn't talk to somebody, but it was fairly late, and she wasn't even sure that she could afford late-night calls. Therapists always said to call anytime, but a bill was always attached. If she really needed her therapist, Keisha would call her and damn the bills, but right now it was more a case of needing the comfort of knowing somebody was there to talk to.

In a weird way, it was also what she had done with Jaxon earlier today. She'd reached out and had been absolutely stunned when he had shown up, looking to help. She knew that he didn't want the divorce since he'd been dragging his heels about signing the papers. She wasn't even sure that she wanted a divorce herself, but she wasn't sure she wanted a marriage right now either. It was too complicated with her sister, and, yes, Keisha deserved a life of her own, but she also couldn't bail on Kelly.

She just couldn't do that right now. Not when Kelly's health was constantly in this precarious situation. Every time she made a step forward and tried to do things, her body seemed to fail her and pushed her back into a wall that neither of them recognized or could see a way through. That just made things all that much harder. Keisha wanted her sister to improve, yet it was hard to see a way forward. That was the reason Keisha had initially gone to see someone to talk her way through all this mess. The trouble was, Keisha hadn't been going recently, and now her work with the animals was keeping her alive and mostly sane.

But what if something happened to her? She had to seriously contemplate what the outcome would be for Kelly. The house would be hers, except that, while Keisha was married, it would probably automatically go to Jaxon. And he probably needed a place too.

Feeling the weight of the world on her shoulders, Keisha quickly turned off the lights, curled up in a ball, and let herself cry. Always silently because the thought of somebody hearing her would never be okay, not now that she was responsible for the care of her sister.

She remembered one of the questions that Jaxon had asked her at one point in time, about whether Kelly even needed care. She was in a wheelchair, but he'd seen so many other people in wheelchairs who lived alone and who took total responsibility for their own daily care. For Keisha, that remark had seemed sacrilegious. Why had he even asked such a thing? Now she was more willing to take a look at the hard facts, and the reality told Keisha that she wasn't sure she could do this for much longer. And, with that fresh perspective, Keisha understood where Jaxon's question had come from.

Her response had been anything but kind, and maybe she was the one responsible for all the ill will in the house at the time the three of them all lived here. She hadn't been aware that Kelly had been insulting and disrespectful to Jaxon. Then Jaxon had his own issues for sure, but he was also her husband. She winced as she realized how many pitfalls she'd slid herself into and hadn't seen a way out. It seemed as if Jaxon had been the final straw that had broken the camel's back, but literally it was probably more like he had been the last straw.

When he had moved out to Timber's place, it had been a massive relief, and yet Keisha didn't feel any better. It was a relief only because the situation at her home had changed and because she could breathe for a moment, but only for a moment because Kelly was still intent on making Keisha's life difficult.

She winced at her own wayward thoughts. However, her sister was still causing trouble, and, whether Keisha was ready to admit it or not, that thought was always right there in the back of her mind. It made sense that Kelly was causing trouble because she was petrified of her own future and couldn't see a way out.

Keisha fell into a deeply troubled sleep. When her phone rang in the middle of the night, she reached out a groggy hand and answered it, only to hear that same mocking laughter in the background. This time, there were words to go with it.

"Are you sure you made the right choice?"

CHAPTER 10

JAXON WOKE UP the next morning, not sure if he should feel optimistic that Keisha had called him yesterday or depressed that she had only called him because she needed help with Kelly. At least Keisha had called him, but, on the other side of things, it didn't seem to help his situation as her husband much.

Still, he wouldn't sit here and get angry when she had needed somebody and when he had been the one she called. Plus, he had been available, so he'd gone. At the same time, it had been good to see her and good to talk to her, just as normal human beings. It also let him see a little bit of her side of the story. What he did see was what he'd seen before, and the fact that she was completely stressed over Kelly was an untenable situation and would be long-term, but he hadn't approached it very well, not realizing just how strong that sisterly bond had been. Yet it wasn't so much a bond as much as it was guilt, at least that was his fear. Something was eating Kelly over this whole thing, and it wasn't an easy subject to broach with Keisha because she'd never been willing to talk to him about Kelly.

When Keisha had given him the ultimatum to move out, he'd been devastated, but, in the typical fashion of those in his world, he had grabbed his few belongings and had gone quickly without a word. The divorce papers had followed almost immediately. As he left, he hadn't seen Kelly at all, but he could almost hear her cheering the demise of his marriage as he left the house. And yet, when it came to Keisha calling and requesting help, he hadn't even hesitated because that's just who he was.

Not necessarily a good thing at this point in time, what with the divorce pending, but he was happy to help. It was hard though. How did you *not* help people whom you loved? And he still loved her; that wasn't the question. He'd come home to her, thinking this was his home, only to find out that it wasn't his home at all. It was *her* home—and her sister's home. It had never been his home, not really. It was all about Kelly, and that wouldn't be something Keisha liked hearing either. It was a tough situation, and he hadn't handled it the best way himself.

He got up, his thoughts heavy as he walked downstairs to the kitchen. He immediately tucked up to the big dining table, realizing that everybody seemed to be here already, and a meal was already being served. "I guess I slept in," he muttered, looking around. "Sorry about that."

Timber looked over at him and shook his head. "No need to apologize. We've all been on the go, no matter who and where we are," he noted, with a laugh.

"Yeah, and there seems to be no end to it."

"That's true. So how is her sister doing?"

Jaxon frowned. "She had apparently fallen, and they kept her at the hospital for quite a while, for observation and some treatments. ... I'm not sure I even want to know what those were. I'm sure it was nothing good, since she's paralyzed."

"Yeah, particularly if she's not maintaining her medications," Timber added. "I've seen more than a few people do that, either as a way to get attention or because depression had set in. All because they just didn't see any way out of the situation they were in."

Jaxon nodded. "Kelly's definitely not a happy person. I'm just not sure that anybody can do anything to change that either."

"Nobody can make her happy if she is not willing to try it herself," Timber noted immediately.

"I understand that too," Jaxon replied.

"Like most of us here already know, when people get so down and so depressed that they need specialized help, they're usually the very ones who won't go get it."

"In Kelly's case, I don't think she would allow anybody to help her. I don't think that's really what she wants."

"You don't think she wants to be helped?" Timber asked curiously.

He was surprised at the instinctive response inside himself. "I think she just wants all this to go away. I think she wants to be back in the world that she had had before the accident. She hasn't been willing to even try to come to terms with the fact that this is her reality now."

"We've all seen that happen too," Dwight interjected, as he sat down beside him, with a plate of his own.

"I'm glad you're eating at least," Timber joked.

"Every time I come in, it seems as if you're the last one to get food," Jaxon noted.

"I often am," Dwight confirmed, with a shrug. "It doesn't matter to me. If you guys are all fed, then you get out of my hair sooner, and I can clean up and go on about my day."

Jaxon smiled at that. "As soon as I grab some coffee, I'll be out of your hair."

Timber looked at him when he came back from refilling his cup. "You think she'll be okay?"

Jaxon pondered that. "Kelly or Keisha? I'm hoping Kelly will be okay," he shared. "It's an odd question to answer regarding Keisha. I feel as if Keisha's at the end of her rope and isn't sure how to progress from one step to the other. She's unsure of everything in her world right now, with no idea how to proceed. She's just majorly overwhelmed."

"I would agree with the overwhelmed part," Dwight added. "I saw her when she was here. Although she was everything that everybody needed her to be," he began, "it was obvious that what she needed was something completely different."

Jaxon nodded. "She seemed incredibly stressed, and I tried to stay out of her way. I didn't want to add to the problem. But my just being here was adding to the problem," he pointed out, with a sigh.

"That's her problem then," Dwight said in a neutral tone of voice.

"I get that too, and we did talk yesterday. It was nice, calm, and peaceful, and she mentioned a couple things that absolutely shocked me. One being that she wasn't quite sure why she started the divorce proceedings."

Both men looked at him in surprise.

"I think it goes along with the fact that she's completely overwhelmed," Jaxon suggested, waving his hands. "I feel as if she doesn't know how to move forward with anything, and she's drowning in the role as her sister's caregiver."

Both Dwight and Timber winced at that and nodded. "And, boy, have we seen that before," Dwight muttered.

"Yeah, I have too, and I don't like to see it in her case. Yet I'm not sure what I'm supposed to do."

"And yet she was fine to talk to?"

"Yes, she was fine, and it was good to talk to her," Jaxon stated, with a smile. "It wasn't the same, and I do understand a little bit more about how this all came about. I do know that I won't sign those divorce papers," he shared, staring off into the distance, "because I don't think that's the answer."

The men gave him an approving look.

"At least don't sign them yet," Timber clarified. "I'm sure she's dealing with other things in her world right now, and that would be her sister."

"Exactly, and I feel for her. I really do. I'm not sure how to help her though."

"I think at this point in time," Timber suggested, "just be there for her. If she calls again, you go. If she doesn't call again, you contact her and suggest maybe going out for a meal, getting back to the reason why you two came together in the first place."

"I was thinking about that," Jaxon admitted, with a nod. "I was not blameless before or even when I got back. In fact, I found it very difficult to be in the same house with Kelly."

"Why is that?"

"She's ..." He frowned. "I know it'll sound terrible, but she's not an easy person to be around, let alone get along with. It was obvious that she didn't want me there, and because I felt I wasn't wanted ..."

"It became a fact," Timber noted, with a groan.

"Yep." Dwight whistled. "I've heard that a time or two."

Jaxon sighed. "It's just frustrating. Keisha asked me to leave. So I left. She sends me the divorce papers, which is the last thing I want," he admitted, looking from Dwight to Timber. "It's absolutely the last thing I want, and yet that's where I'm at."

Timber asked, "Does she want to go through with the divorce?"

"It doesn't sound like it to me," Dwight remarked.

"No, I don't think she does," Jaxon agreed, "but we've just not gotten anywhere yet."

"No, you're everywhere," Timber noted. "You're not in a bad place at all, especially since you're talking now. Give her some time. I can see how you coming home made things between you and Keisha already different. Then you're having trouble with the sister, and the sister's having trouble with you, and it's quite possible that Keisha was caught right in the middle and didn't have a clue how to handle the strife between the two of you."

"And that's very possible too," Jaxon acknowledged, thinking about it. "I'll just give Kelly some space."

"I think space is the perfect answer," Timber replied. "So now you can just settle back here and be available in case anything else happens. It's a really good sign that Keisha reached out to you when she needed someone."

As he got up, he turned to Timber and added, "There is one more thing. She's also in some sort of mess."

"What kind?"

"The online kind. Apparently, it happened just as I was deployed last time," he explained. "She started getting an awful lot of really nasty social media stuff and was being plagued by nasty spam phone calls, that kind of thing. I've just recently started getting them myself, and I learned today that she is too. Even though she no longer has social media accounts, she's getting that same nasty mocking computerized voice that comes on when she answers her phone, just like me."

The two men frowned at him, and he nodded.

"The fact that it's both of us? … That's not random. It can't be. Not if it's both of us at the same time. It makes no sense."

"And she has no family?"

"No, just the sister."

"Do you know the circumstances of the car accident?"

"It killed her parents. I know that much," Jaxon clarified, "but I don't know any more than that." When Timber frowned, Jaxon noted the look on his face. "Why?"

"I just wondered if something else was going on with that accident, and somebody just can't leave you guys to live your lives."

He shrugged. "I don't even know what to say to that, but I can tell you that I don't have any answers, and neither does Keisha. In fact, I got several of the spam phone calls while I was at the restaurant with her, which is what brought up the conversation for us." Jaxon shrugged. "It's just so weird."

"Yeah, … that's past weird," Dwight noted.

"How many of these are you getting in a day?" Timber asked.

"At the moment, I would say a couple, and sometimes it's worse. Sometimes it's steady, and I just shut off my phone because what else do you do?" he asked, with a wry look. "It's almost impossible to sort out who it is, but you know that it's got to be somebody. Hopefully it won't be anybody we know." Timber frowned at him, and Jaxon shrugged. "I just can't help getting past the feeling that because the two of us are getting the same type calls, it has to be somebody who knows us both, which is incredibly unnerving," he declared, staring at him.

"And what would be the motive?" Timber asked.

"I don't know. I'm at a complete loss. Unless it's connected to Kelly's accident. Maybe someone feels she has no right to more. To be happy."

Timber added, "As her husband it would make sense to target you too."

Dwight asked, "Have you considered what would happen if anything happens to you?"

"What do you mean?"

"Like your assets, benefits, your estate."

"Oh, yeah. Everything goes to Keisha."

"And what happens if Keisha passes on?"

He winced. "I don't know. I presume in her world everything goes to Kelly, and, because we're divorcing, that's what it would look like anyway, so …"

"Right …"

"Why? It's not as if anybody killing us will benefit anyone."

Dwight nodded. "I get that. It was just a question."

Jaxon stared at Dwight. "It's just a question, but it doesn't feel random."

He smiled. "It's just that old suspicious nature of mine."

"I hear you, but, if you have any suggestions or anything that would make any sense of this, please speak up."

"I will," he said immediately. "Yet, for the moment, I don't have anything, so let's get our asses back to work."

CHAPTER 11

K EISHA MANAGED TO wait several days, half expecting Jaxon to call, then realized he wasn't likely to, not when she and Kelly were initiating all the negativity going on. Keisha finally reached out to him, and, when he didn't answer, she felt a sense of relief. She would leave a message and then decided she didn't know what to say, so she quickly disconnected.

When her phone rang not too much later, he was on the other end. "You called?"

She sighed. "I did, and then I didn't know what to leave for a message, so I just … didn't."

"Yeah, I got that part already," he replied, with a note of humor. "Your number is still in my phone."

"Right, … of course it is," she muttered, feeling foolish. "I was just …"

"Coffee maybe?" he asked in that same calm tone.

"Yes, that would be great."

"I'm coming into town later," he explained, amusement now in his tone. "Do you want to make it dinner?"

She hesitated briefly and then replied, "That would be awesome."

"Perfect. I'll meet you at the clinic. It'll probably be closer to five. Is that okay?"

"Yeah, that's good because I've got more than enough to

deal with myself."

"Okay."

And, with those plans set, she headed off to work. When she ran home later during lunch, Kelly was particularly irritable. "Now what is wrong?" Keisha asked. "It's noon, and you know I've got to get back."

"You don't need to stop by at noon every day," Kelly spat bitterly. "I'm not an invalid."

Keisha took a slow calming breath and replied, "No, you're not an invalid, but you did have a recent fall, and I'm not comfortable leaving you alone, especially if stopping by could help save your life."

"Why would you even want to save this life?" Kelly asked bitterly. "It's not one worth living."

The breath whooshed out of Keisha, and she stared at her sister, wondering if she was suicidal. It was one thing to talk about it and to use it for attention, but it was another thing with that note of absolute desperation in Kelly's tone. Keisha tried to analyze what she had heard, but it had come out so fast she wasn't sure that she understood what her sister was even saying. "Do you want to see the therapist again?"

"No, I do not need more therapy," Kelly snapped, her voice rising in anger. "God, that's the last thing I need." She glared as she shouted out, "You know what I need? I need to get out of this freaking wheelchair. I need a life!"

Keisha frowned at that and then nodded. "I agree, and that would be absolutely awesome, but I don't know how to make that happen. So, when you figure it out, Kel, just let me know, and I'll do everything I can to support you." With that, she walked out of the house. As she got in her car and drove back to the clinic, she hadn't told her sister she wouldn't be home for dinner.

She sent her a text when she got back in the office. **I'll be home late tonight.** And she left it at that. Whether Kelly approved or not was a whole different story, and Kelly would definitely not approve of Keisha going out to eat with Jaxon. And that was just one more of those things that she had to deal with between her sister and Jaxon. Although Jaxon appeared to have shifted in many ways, she knew without a doubt that Kelly and Jaxon would rub each other raw, and it would be a challenge to have them in the same room anymore. Her sister had made it very plain when he'd come back that she didn't like having him there, and that it was half her house, which it wasn't, not technically anyway. However, it was Kelly's home, and that mattered.

Yet Keisha was unaware that Kelly had been mean to Jaxon, who was already dealing with his own demons, and the whole thing had put Keisha right in the middle again, leaving her completely overwhelmed and exhausted. As she got back to work, the challenges of the day filled her mind, leaving room for nothing else. When she realized it was five, and she headed for the reception area, she found Jaxon standing there, talking to her receptionist.

Tania looked up with a beaming smile. "Your husband is here."

Keisha's heart lurched, but she nodded normally she hoped and smiled at him. "I just need to lock up."

"Good enough," he said. "Good enough," he said. "I thought I could drive and either take you home after dinner or bring you back here."

She didn't have a problem with that. Particularly as it seemed silly for both of them to drive.

As they walked out together, he asked, "You didn't tell them about the divorce?"

"No, I haven't told anybody, and it's not exactly final, is it?" she asked, with a wry look in his direction.

"I have the papers," he shared, "so I guess, as soon as I sign them, it's final."

"Yeah," she muttered, not sure what to do with that comment. "That would probably complete it, but I don't know. Maybe it has to be filed with the courts or something. I've never been divorced before."

He chuckled. "I was never married before either."

"No, me neither," she agreed, "and we probably were way too fast on that."

"I don't know about that," he countered. "I think we were in love, and now maybe it's time to get to know each other instead."

When she looked over at him in surprise, he shrugged. "It seems to be a good idea to me."

CHAPTER 12

JAXON NOTED HOW Keisha didn't say anything for the rest of the ride, so he just waited to see if she would bring it up or would even contemplate it. She had looked surprised at the idea, but he realized—with his rough homecoming, him still dealing with his injuries and his own struggles, and her inability to come see him while he recovered—it had all been a recipe for disaster. Now he realized that her resistance probably came from much deeper psychological issues based around Kelly and having to deal with her. The idea of having to deal with two invalids in transition was a lot, and the fact that he and Kelly didn't get along, guaranteeing constant drama and conflict, may have been the final straw.

He understood more now and noted he hadn't been very thoughtful at the time. He just showed up back home, probably a little harder and a little darker, a little brusque, potentially needy. That image made him wince just thinking about it. That was not who he was, but seeing the situation when he arrived made it particularly difficult for him, and he already knew he hadn't handled it well. Now he would try and backpedal as much as he could.

When he drove up to their favorite restaurant, she looked at it and nodded. "I haven't been here since."

"Me neither," he confirmed, with a smile. "So, let's go in

and see if the food is still as good."

He acted completely cool about it, not wanting to put any significance into this choice, but a part of him had driven here on purpose. This was a place they had spent many happy nights getting to know each other, but apparently that was before the shit hit the fan, and now everything was different. He just hadn't expected there to be such a huge difference this time around.

As they walked in, he gave the waitress his name for their reservation, and they were quickly led to a table off to the side.

She smiled as she realized it was even the same table. "Did you ask for this?"

"No, I did not," he replied, with a note of laughter. "Yet it's interesting that they gave it to us."

They ordered quickly, both already knowing the menu, and, when they were finally left alone again, he looked over at her and smiled. "How was your day?"

She gave half a snort. "This is completely surreal, you asking me about my day, as if we're back to some semblance of a normal relationship," she muttered, just shaking her head. "That just takes the cake."

He shrugged. "No reason *not* to ask how your day was," he noted. "I worked with llamas all day."

She flushed. "And I tend to forget that you're out there doing something too."

"In this case I was, though I don't know how successfully," he clarified, with half a laugh, "but I was trying. I also worked at the bunkhouse for a while, as we finished setting up a large bathroom shower area and then connected it to the septic."

"Ooh, that sounds like a fun job," she teased.

Then he laughed. "On the other hand, not only do we have a place for everybody to sleep, now we're set up for everybody to shower, and that is a huge thing."

"I can't imagine what bunkhouse living is like," she shared. "Yet it sounds like something I would really enjoy."

"You would for a while because it's different, and then you would want some spare time and freedom, and a little more private space," he noted, with a laugh. "You've had your own place for a number of years, so that could be hard to switch out from."

"Maybe," she murmured.

"It is your house, isn't it?" he asked her.

She looked over at him and shrugged. "Yeah, it is."

They fell silent for a long moment, and then he added, "I never meant for you to feel as if you had to choose, you know?"

Startled, she looked over at him. "What are you talking about?"

"I didn't want you to feel as if you had to choose between us, … between me and Kelly."

She blinked several times and then flushed. "Which … I guess I already did, didn't I?"

"Exactly," he said, but he tried hard to keep the rancor out of his tone. He'd been working through a lot of stuff recently, and this appeared to be just one more thing that needed to be dealt with. He added, "I'm sorry if that's how I made you feel. That wasn't my intent."

She stared off in the distance. "I don't know if it was a case of making me feel that way or not," she replied. "I knew you were coming, and, while you were in the process of returning, Kelly had several bad falls, and it was triggering an awful lot of things, and a sense of loss over my parents' deaths that I didn't realize I hadn't dealt with. Every time Kelly fell or had another setback, it just brought everything up again about the car accident. You hadn't been here to see it or to deal with it for most of those years since Kel's accident. So, when you came home, it suddenly just seemed as if we were strangers."

He nodded. "And I didn't help anything by not getting along with her."

"She's not been the easiest to get along with," she admitted cautiously, "and lately it's been even worse."

"I'm sorry. That's hard. You never get a break from being a caregiver."

"No"—she laughed—"but it's really not like being a real caregiver. Anybody with a family member who has extra needs, there's no breaks for them either."

"There is sometimes," he added, "but it depends on individual circumstances, I guess."

Their first course arrived just after that, giving them a bit of a break from the heavy topic of conversation. He tried to interject more of a light and easy *getting to know each other* tone. "How about the knitting?" he asked suddenly.

He watched as she looked up at him, startled. Her eyes widened, and she started to giggle. "Yeah, that whole thing went in the garbage."

His eyebrows shot up. "Yet you were really proud of what you were doing."

"That didn't last very long," she muttered. "I don't know what happened, but all of a sudden I had more stitches than I started with, and everything started to go sideways … literally." She laughed. "I tried to fix it, made it worse, tried to fix it again, and finally ended up just deciding that really wasn't my thing."

He grinned at her. "Dang, I really loved the idea of you sitting at home knitting," he shared, with a chuckle. "It was such a fun thing to envision."

"I was trying to find things that would give me more downtime, more rest, you know? Things that would give me something else to occupy my mind with, yet allowing my body to calm down. That's what hobbies are supposed to be for, right?"

"Maybe," he conceded, with a smirk. "I think people have hobbies for a lot of different reasons, but the few times I heard about the knitting, you sounded as if you were really happy with it."

"Yeah, … that didn't last," she said, still snickering. "But, hey, I tried, and that's what counts."

"It does count," he agreed immediately. "It counts a lot, and I'm just sorry I didn't get to see it."

She pulled out her phone and spent a few moments swiping through her pictures, then held it up. "This is what it looked like."

As he took the phone from her, he saw the front of the misshapen garment hanging sideways, like a drunken sailor, and he started to laugh.

"Yeah, that's what I was doing too," she replied. "It was so bad."

"It's a pretty good conversation piece," he noted, trying to hold back his laughter.

"Yeah, well, I didn't think I needed to invest months of frustration to create *that*."

He just grinned at her, still smiling. "I think it's great that you tried."

"Maybe one day, when I'm old and gray, sitting in a rocking chair, I'll try again, but, for now, it won't happen."

At that, he burst out laughing, and the conversation got a little bit easier from then on. By the time they finished eating and were both sitting back, enjoying the relaxed glow of good food and good company, she asked, "Did you ever pick up any other hobbies?"

"I do a ton of woodworking," he noted, with a shrug. "But right now it's more work than hobby because I'm doing a lot of that for Timber, but I'm also doing an awful lot of … everything. So right now, I'm just trying to work as hard as I can, and, if I have any energy at the end of the day, I go visit the animals. Something is so incredibly healing about being out there with them."

"That," she declared, "I can agree with totally. Animals are so great for that. It's been the animals who have held me together through so much over the last decade."

"Has it been that long?" he asked, turning to face her.

She frowned as she thought about it. "It's not been a decade since the accident, if that's what you're asking. However, as you know, becoming a vet was a challenge," she shared, with a wry smile, "and expensive. There were certainly plenty of days that I went to bed crying. And honestly, it still happens from time to time. Setting up my own practice wasn't easy, and I still have days when I wonder if I've done the right thing. I don't know," she admitted, with a smile. "It seems as if life gives us twists and turns, and whether we can navigate and stay on our feet matters," she suggested, giving him a look. "Otherwise it can get very difficult."

"I hear you there," he confirmed. "I didn't expect to end up with a prosthetic. I didn't expect to end up injured at all." Then he winced and added, "And I sure didn't expect to wind up divorced."

"That's what life does to you," she said immediately and then frowned as she stared down at her glass of wine.

"It is," he acknowledged, glossing it over and changing the subject a bit. "So, is business good? Are you happy with having your own practice? Is there enough business for the two clinics?"

"I'm happy having my own clinic," she replied. "Business is up and down, but most of the time it's good. It just needs to be steady enough that I can keep the staff employed. That is the one thing that keeps me up in the middle of the night."

"How so?"

"It's just worrying when I pay the bills at the end of the day, wondering if I have enough money to go around, or do I need to be raising prices, which would hurt a lot of my clients who just don't have it. Then I wonder if I should find another way to make more money, you know, a side hustle," she added, with a smile. "And, no, I don't have a clue what that would be. For the most part, everything is going fine. Then, once in a while, we'll have a month where things are not so great, and I'll start worrying again. Until the next month—when I can pay for everything, and it looks better— so I relax a little. It just goes in cycles."

"I can see that," he said and nodded.

"I'm not so well established yet that I don't have to worry about it nor so overwhelmingly popular with clients that I'm turning people away," she pointed out. "I can't imagine what that would feel like either because, to me, turning somebody away if their pet is in need is something I can't do."

"Agreed. We don't want to be doing that."

"So, what about your family?" When he looked at her

quizzically, she flushed. "I'm sure I'm supposed to know, but I've honestly forgotten."

"My dad passed away while I was deployed this last time," he shared. "I did tell you, but I think it happened at the point in time that you were dealing with your sister having seizures."

Visibly embarrassed, she moaned. "Honest to God, I don't remember you telling me."

"I did, but …" Then he just shrugged.

"I feel like so much of my life has gotten washed away while dealing with Kelly, but then I feel completely guilty for saying that since I have a healthy life, and she's in a wheelchair and can't do very much," she explained. "And then I circle back around again."

"I'm sure those are the common guilt feelings anybody would have."

"Maybe," she murmured, "I don't know. Anyway, I'm sorry about your dad. I don't even remember you telling me that."

"I left a message with your sister."

She frowned at him. "And then you never mentioned it again?"

"I did, but I think you were distracted at the time because you cut me off about something else."

"Oh, crap," she muttered, staring at him in shock.

He shrugged, feeling some of the hurt from back then ease slightly. "Yeah." He smiled at her. "It was a rough time."

"Did you … did you get time off, to go see them?"

"I did," he replied, eyeing her strangely.

She frowned at him. "This is another one of those things where you'll tell me that you told me about it too, but I didn't respond, isn't it?"

"Yeah, that's pretty much it," he confirmed and frowned. "Kind of reminds me of you feeling we are strangers."

"And yet how?" She stopped, then added in frustration, "I don't know how I would have missed that news."

"I don't know either," he admitted. "But afterward, I didn't really mention it because you had been fairly distant about it. Maybe that was part of my resentment over the lack of communication, and then, when I got home, it's like everything was about Kelly."

"You really were jealous of her?"

He winced at that and said, "I really hate to think that's the case, but I've come to understand that I've been envious coming home to find that she got your attention and that I got divorce papers." Her breath caught up at that. As she stared at him, he nodded. "So, I guess that's some of my issues, but that's not why we're here."

"No, it's not, but you're making me realize that I may not have been there for you very much in the marriage." He gave her a hooded look, not sure how to respond to that.

She just blinked several times, as if she was just becoming aware of things that had affected him so badly when she didn't even respond back then. "I honestly don't remember those conversations."

"Like I mentioned, you were in a hard place, with Kelly and with me," he pointed out. "So, I'm not really surprised."

She stared off in the distance, and he watched as she started to shake her head, almost as if she couldn't stop.

"Easy, easy, easy," he said. He quickly called for the bill, realizing that she was one step away from breaking down, so he rushed her out to his vehicle. They sat in the parking lot as he tried to calm her down. "Take it easy. Just breathe."

When she finally calmed down, she looked at him, her eyes wide and bewildered. When he pulled her into his arms and just held her, she broke down, probably for the first time in a very long time.

She just sobbed and sobbed and sobbed.

CHAPTER 13

WHEN KEISHA FINALLY caught her breath, she looked up at him. "I am so sorry," she whispered.

"Hey, it's okay," he told her, a smile on his face. "You've probably been holding those tears for a very long time."

She looked at him and then slowly nodded. "But I'm also so sorry about your family. I somehow didn't register any of that, which was so insensitive."

"And that just shows you how crazy your life has been. Something like that would have never gotten by you normally, or you would have figured it out."

She just blinked and nodded. "I didn't figure it out, didn't hear it, and honestly … I'm not so sure Kelly even told me."

"And I don't know that she did either," he shared. "I did mention it to her a couple times too."

"And I remember you saying something, and me being a little confused. At the time, I didn't think he had just died. I think when you mentioned it, I was already so far out of the loop that I assumed he had passed on a long time ago."

"He didn't." Jaxon shrugged. "Now it was a while ago."

She shook her head. "It's a while ago for you, but apparently I am just hearing about it now."

His lips twitched. "Apparently, and it just goes to show how stressed and overwhelmed you've been."

"And that is absolutely no excuse," she declared, staring at him. "I went through so much when my parents passed, and I am horrified that I just ignored your trauma."

"And maybe it was a coping mechanism," he suggested. "I wasn't terribly close to him, but it certainly hurt in ways that I don't even want to go into now."

"Of course, and I remember you saying you weren't close," she added, frowning as she stared off in the distance. "But that's not the same thing as being okay to lose them."

"No, it sure isn't," he confirmed and still smiled. "Anyway, I did fly home for a couple days, went through the arrangements and all, and took care of clearing out my dad's apartment. I did actually hire a company to clear it out, and that was about it. He didn't want a big service. He just wanted to be cremated and to have his ashes scattered over the land," he shared. "So I went to my grandmother's farm and did just that."

She smiled and nodded. "That's not a bad idea."

"It's not allowed in every state though," he pointed out. "Thankfully it worked out the way he wanted."

"Of course," she murmured. "My parents didn't want funerals either, but everybody kept telling me that, if I didn't, I wasn't honoring them."

"I don't know about that," he argued. "I think their wishes should have some meaning, but you have to make it work for the living as well."

"Kelly says that because we have the monument, it's a place she can go mourn."

"And does she?" he asked.

She turned to him and then shook her head. "No, she doesn't go anywhere. I drag her out of the house to go shopping once in a while, but she screams and howls and makes a scene. It's not worth it."

"And then she becomes too housebound, and her world has narrowed to the first floor—or at least her bedroom and your living room."

"Yeah, and not even the kitchen hardly," she added. "She's not eating very much, and, when she does eat, she invariably wants something other than what I've cooked." He just stared at her, and she shrugged. "I think it's all part and parcel of the depression, part of the … *my life sucks* mantra of hers." She gave a hearty sigh. "And then there's me. I'm healthy. I have my own practice. I have absolutely no reason to be feeling anything other than grateful."

"Which is what you use to trash yourself all the more," he pointed out, "because that's a comparison that isn't easy to turn around. It's like survivor's guilt, hard to release yourself from the blame of."

"No, it isn't," she agreed, "and that makes it even worse."

He laughed. "You always were the kind to blame yourself if you couldn't fix things."

She winced and nodded. "Apparently."

"No *apparently* about it," he declared. "And I got over my distress when I realized just how overwhelmed you were. Sure, I was upset for a while, feeling as if my family didn't matter, but yours apparently did."

Her breath caught in the back of her throat, and she stared at him and started to shake again.

"Easy. I'm not saying these things to hurt you."

"And yet you're doing a hell of a good job."

He winced. "You're right. I just need to stop talking."

"No, you don't," she said in frustration, "because I didn't know. I had no idea of the loss that you've been going through."

"I did tell Kelly to tell you, and I did mention it later to her and to you."

"Did you mention it in a way that, if I hadn't heard the news, I would have understood, or did you just say something because you were hurting?"

He sighed. "I have no idea. And it doesn't matter now. That part is definitely over with."

"Maybe for you," she muttered, "but it doesn't feel like it's over for me."

"I'm sorry," he said. "I wasn't trying to bring all that up, but it was something that I struggled with and didn't understand why the loss of my father didn't matter."

"It did matter," she stated immediately. She shook her head, as if not sure what to say or do. "Could you just take me home? I think I've had enough truth bombs for the night. Right now I feel like I should have driven home instead of leaving my car at the clinic."

"I'll take you back to the clinic to get it." Without a word, he turned on the engine. As he drove, he added, "I don't want to leave us like this, on such a sour note."

"No, no, I'm fine." Then she gave a broken laugh. "Obviously I'm not fine, but it's a little hard to see myself through your eyes and face the reality of what I missed. And maybe for good reasons or bad," she noted, "but I look back, and it just highlights …"

"It highlights," he interjected, "how overwhelmed you were then and how overwhelmed you still are."

She shot him a look and then nodded. "But it doesn't matter because I can't get out of this life that I'm in." And, with that, as they pulled up to her clinic, she hopped out and turned to him. "Thanks for dinner."

Then she quickly got into her car and drove off.

CHAPTER 14

K EISHA WOKE THE next morning, feeling as if she'd been dragged over hot coals all night. She was blaming herself, and she understood that, but damn it hurt. She truly didn't remember anything about Jaxon's father passing. After she woke up in the middle of the night, she'd gone back through their text messages from years and years ago. And, sure enough, she found a short terse one, where he'd shared that his father had passed away and that he needed to go home. He would be taking leave, and he would contact her when he got stateside. There was not even a responding text from her.

When he contacted her again by text a little later, it had been another short message, saying that he was dealing with his family issues, and he would contact her later. And she'd given him a thumbs-up.

He'd lost his father, and she'd given him a thumbs-up?

She sat here, hugging a cup of coffee in the morning, wondering what the hell had happened to her world. And yet she knew that, ever since the accident, when her parents had passed and her sister had been injured, Keisha hadn't even had a chance to catch a break.

She managed to finish her degree and had set up her own practice, all while everything had blown up around her. And what had she done in response? She'd blown up her own marriage.

When she heard Kelly slowly wheel her way into the kitchen, Keisha looked over at Kelly and asked, "How was your night?"

"Pretty shitty. The least you could have done was tell me you went out on a date with him," she grumbled.

Such venom filled her sister's tone, Keisha stared at her in shock. "It wasn't a date. It was a conversation, and divorces require that, you know?"

"No, they don't. They require conversations with lawyers," she snapped, then wheeled over and poured herself a cup of coffee. "You did not need to go out with him in any way, shape, or form."

Keisha stared at her sister for a long moment, not even sure what to say, still dealing with her own issues. "Did you know that his dad died?"

Kelly looked at her and smiled. "Yeah, so did you."

"Are you sure about that? He said that he told you and left a message for me."

"Oh, did he now?" she asked, with an eye roll. "That's nice and convenient for him, isn't it? And for you too, so you don't have to acknowledge that you didn't give a crap."

She stared at her sister. "Are you saying that I was so cold and disinterested in him that I didn't give a crap that his father died?" she asked, staring at her sister, trying to figure out just what this was all about.

"I sure won't mention it," she snapped, setting the cup down hard. "We had enough on our plate at the time."

"Yes, we did, and part of that was you having multiple sessions where you had to go to the hospital, as I recall."

"Yeah." Kelly rolled her eyes. "Believe me that I remember."

And that same bitterness filled her tone. Keisha wasn't sure what to do about it. How did one handle that? She didn't say anything and just took another sip of coffee.

Kelly looked at her. "I never did tell you."

"You never did tell me what?"

"I never did tell you that his dad died, but … I'm pretty damn sure he texted you about it."

"Yeah, he did, and I didn't see it," Keisha noted. "He texted me a couple times, and I didn't realize they were related to his dad having died. The texts didn't spell that out, and I didn't scroll up to look. But then again, you didn't pass on the telephone message either."

"No, I sure didn't. I can't stand him, and, if his dad died, … well, sorry about that, but you didn't need one more thing on your plate."

At that moment, Keisha realized the level of selfishness her sister exhibited was completely off the wall and had probably been the norm all this time. "Are you saying that you deliberately didn't let me know because you were afraid it would distract me from looking after you?"

Kelly looked at her, a funny expression on her face, and then shrugged. "I don't know, and I guess we'll never find out, since it's over with, and his parents are both dead and gone."

It was such a callous attitude that Keisha stared at her. "Yeah, they are, and that's one of the reasons he was not in great shape when he got here, since he was hanging on to that resentment."

"That's his problem," Kelly declared. "He's an adult. He can deal with it."

Keisha stared at her sister. "He lost his father. Did you not hear me?"

"Yeah, I get it, but, if you'd read your text messages, you would have known. It just goes to show you that you weren't really that interested in his life since you weren't even reading his messages."

"I did read his messages. I just missed the one above," she explained. "I read that family issues were going on, but I never at any point in time saw the text where it spelled out that his dad had passed on. The fact that he phoned and left a message with you that you deliberately didn't tell me about is something I'm really struggling with."

"Of course you are," Kelly spat bitterly. "As soon as he comes back into your life, you're just this big old mess," she snapped. "Everything was just fine without him."

"Oh, I don't know about that. I don't know how fine any of it is," Keisha replied.

"It's way better than when he was here."

"He said that you were really rude to him."

She looked over at her and snorted. "Apparently not rude enough, since he didn't leave until you finally gave him the boot." She stared her down. "I figured that, if he wasn't around, then things could get back to normal."

Keisha winced. "Seriously?"

"Yeah, seriously. I don't even know what you saw in him in the first place."

She stared at Kelly. "It doesn't matter if you knew what I saw in him or not. You should have been happy that I found someone to share my life with."

"Right, I'm supposed to be happy for you because you found someone, when I'll never find anyone myself."

"So, what then? I'm not allowed to be happy because you can't be happy either?" she asked, staring at her sister. "Is that what this is all about?"

"No, of course not," she muttered, with a wave of her hand. "God, that's not my thing at all."

And yet Kelly's tone had been slightly off, and it stuck with Keisha throughout the day.

When she finally had time for a breather at the clinic, one of her assistants looked over at her and said, "I know you keep saying everything is fine, and you don't want to talk about it, but something is definitely riding you. You've been working us all incredibly hard today."

She blinked as she stared at her, then looked back around at Tania, the receptionist, who nodded.

"And we're happy to help," Eva added, with a shake of her head. "We obviously know some issues are going on, but if your ex is causing you this much stress, it's no wonder you're getting divorced."

Tania looked at her and asked, "You're divorcing him? I told you that your husband was here just yesterday," she pointed out, with a frown. "How come you didn't correct me?"

"Because we're not divorced yet," she clarified and looked over at the two of them, as they both stared expectantly.

"So ..." Eva added, with an exaggerated sigh.

Keisha shrugged. "I guess it's really my sister I don't know what to do with."

The two of them looked at each other, then at her. "That's a tough one."

"It's more than a tough one," Keisha acknowledged, with a nod. "I found out something last night, after having dinner with my ex, my husband, ... Jesus, I don't even know what to call him."

"What did you find out?" Tania asked.

"In the course of having dinner with Jaxon," she began, "I found out that I had missed a text from him telling me that his dad had died."

Both of them just stared at her.

"I know, not exactly something that you miss. But he had texted follow-up messages after that, and I read those but I didn't scroll up, so I missed the real context," she shared. "He hadn't called because he was deployed overseas with no phone available, and, then when he did phone, he left a message with Kelly."

"Right, well, that was probably his next-best option."

"She didn't tell me about his message."

Silence.

That bombshell had both of them staring at her in shock.

Keisha nodded. "So, last night I casually asked him about his family. His mother died of cancer some time ago, which I remembered, but his dad apparently died while he had been on his last tour overseas, which I should have already known about. … So you can imagine how that went over."

"Oh, God."

"Jesus."

They both stole a glance at each other and then refocused on her. "Why did your sister not tell you?" Eva asked.

"For one thing, at the time, she'd had multiple falls, and things were not great. Plus, she apparently hated him. She hated him back then and hates him even more now."

"And she didn't tell you that his dad had died?"

"No, she deliberately didn't tell me," she repeated. "She left me to find out all on my own. So, I apologize for running you ragged today. I'm honestly still in a bit of shock.

Not only is that screw-up definitely on me, but I hadn't realized the inattention I've shown Jaxon during our marriage while he wasn't here. And, while I knew Kelly wasn't a fan, I had no idea the level of disregard or hate she's had for him all this time."

"That's a tough one," Tania noted, visible shaking. "My God, to not tell you that his father had died, leaving you to completely miss showing any support for him? … What a mess."

"I know. Believe me that I know. Jaxon told me that he's over it and that he did text me to say that he was staying to handle the issues that needed to be handled, and then he was deployed again. He did say it was one of the things that he really struggled with."

They just stared at her. Eva nodded. "Of course he did. The loss of a parent is hard. You know that, and so does Kelly. How can that be something that anybody doesn't confirm until it's clear?"

"I think on his part, when I didn't respond and prioritized my sister's care over his needs, that put a nail in the proverbial coffin, so he quit trying to communicate with me. I don't even want to think about him dealing with his injuries on his own."

"And yet he's not the one who wants a divorce?" Tania asked, bewildered.

Keisha looked over at her in surprise and then slowly shook her head. "No, he's not the one who wants a divorce."

She thought about it a lot later that day and that night because it really was shocking how this had all played out. Jaxon wasn't the one looking for the divorce, but how badly did she want to get away from the situation?

A better question was, did she love him?

Did he love her?

And, if he did, were they willing to fight for that love?

He was, but she'd already said no, and that was the problem. She'd said no by asking for the divorce, and yet she knew in her heart of hearts that divorce was basically her exit strategy for a caregiving life with her sister that had gotten very difficult. Keisha didn't know how to handle Kelly anymore, and marrying Jaxon hadn't turned out to be the escape route she thought it would be or that it could have been. Because she owned the house and they moved into it because of her sister, it had just made things that much worse.

Not liking the snapshot into her own personality right now, Keisha went home, had leftovers, offered Kelly some, ignored her when she refused, then went out for a walk. She had the dogs with her, and it took a little bit for her to calm down enough to find some clarity in all the confusion. She didn't think much of herself right now, and she owed Jaxon a pretty major apology. Not only had she *not* treated him like a partner, she had treated him as an inconvenience, somebody causing her trouble, instead of somebody there to discuss her troubles with and to help her find another solution.

She groaned as she walked, loud and irritated, which caused a couple other people out walking to turn to her.

She shrugged at one and just said, "It's been one of those days."

The woman laughed. "Sometimes I think it's one of those years."

And wasn't that the truth? Even as she walked, Keisha felt the need to apologize and the need to find clarity with Jaxon. She pulled out her phone, and, not giving herself a chance to question it and to back out, she called him. When he answered, his voice was distracted. "Hey, am I calling at a bad time?"

"No, not at all," he replied. "Hang on a sec. I'll just step outside."

"If you don't mind, I would appreciate that." Then she hesitated and added, "If you have a moment, I would just like to talk, if you have privacy."

"Sure," he said, his voice calm.

It was that same steadiness that she realized she really missed. It had been the part of him that she'd always appreciated and had relied on. When he'd returned from his last tour, he'd been a bit of a mess, coming into a household where she was a mess as well, and her sister was even a bigger mess.

"I owe you an apology," she began abruptly.

There was silence on the other end and then a chuckle. "I'm not sure why you would." There wasn't any sense of *Yeah, you do* or anything else. It was more curiosity. "What is it you think you've done that you owe me an apology for?"

"Lots of things," she began. "I don't know if I can even get it all clear in my head, but I'm working on it."

"Maybe you should tell me then."

She tried to explain, and some of her words got muddled, but some of it came out okay. Finally she stopped talking. She had rambled long enough and had probably made it worse. "I think I butchered that more than I clarified anything," she added, with a groan.

"No, I think you did pretty well," he replied. "First off, I do not hold anything about the loss of my father against you. I won't lie. Your response was hurtful at the time. It's clear that Kelly was obviously having issues at the time, and she was alive and clearly took precedence over those already deceased," he shared and sighed. "I had always wondered if your sister had given you the message, and, once I got back home again, I realized she probably hadn't. It's one of the reasons I've had so little patience with her, but that's also on me."

"No, it's not on you," she argued, her tone hard. "Part of the reason I didn't have any tolerance or patience with you was because I was already really struggling with looking after her. I feel guilty as hell, and I don't know what the solution is, but instead of asking for suggestions or involving you in finding a solution, I made you part of the problem and never gave you a chance, and, for that, I'm also sorry."

Silence came for a long moment, and he finally spoke. "I appreciate that. I hadn't considered it from that point of view, but I can see how that might have come about. At the risk of pissing you off," he added, with a dry laugh, "I do think you need to come up with a different solution for Kelly because honestly, this doesn't appear to be a healthy scenario for either one of you."

"No, it sure isn't," she confirmed. "I made dinner tonight, and once again she wouldn't eat. I just walked out because I don't know what else to do."

"I think it's something you may need to get professional help with," he suggested. "I'm not telling you that she needs to move out, but I am worried that the situation is not healthy for her. She's become extremely dependent on you, and, given her circumstances, I can see why," he said immediately. "I'm not saying you need to get rid of your sister, but she needs to sort out her own life, on her own."

"That's good," she noted, an odd note of humor in her tone, "because that's obviously not an option."

"No, it may not be a financial option, and I get that," he stated, with a sigh, "but what also isn't great is that you are spending your entire life looking after her, and I don't see any evidence of gratitude from her."

"Me neither."

"She's still the same?"

"More or less."

"Then she needs an intervention. She's still so angry and keeps herself busy making your life miserable, so you are suffering as well," he stated. "That needs to stop."

"Needs to stop," she repeated, her voice cracking. "I've done a lot of soul searching these last couple days, but honestly, I don't have any idea how to make it better, let alone stop it completely," she admitted.

"I don't know either," he conceded, "but it's time for you to have some serious conversations with her."

"And yet she has no place else to go. This is her home, and I certainly can't just kick her out," she pointed out.

"And I'm not saying that you should, not at all. I understand where she's at, and she needs to know that she has your support, but she also needs to understand that she's basically killing you, and that's not fair either."

"That's a bit melodramatic," Keisha replied.

"Is it?" he asked, deepening his voice. "Is it really?"

"I don't know." She sounded miserable.

"Not from where I'm standing, and I think you know it all too well. It looks as if everything else in your life will go to pot as you try to keep things at home stable for her, and it's still not stable," he noted. "This isn't a criticism at all, but you're not handling it very well anymore. It's cumulative, and I'm sure there's a word for it, something like *caretaker overwhelm-ness*."

She snorted at that. "I highly doubt that's a real term."

"Maybe not," he said, with a laugh. "Maybe it should be."

"Anyway, I do know what you're saying," she admitted, "and, to a certain extent at least, I understand your concern." She frowned as she stared off in the distance and missed what he said next. "What did you say? Sorry, I was off thinking about what to do."

"I guess while you're thinking about what to do, maybe you should ask yourself what you really want to do about me while you're at it."

There was silence at first. "I honestly don't know. I don't know what to say, and I don't know what to do."

"Then do nothing right now," he suggested. "Give yourself a chance to just breathe. That's if you love me. And, if you don't love me anymore, then that's easy. But if you do or if you're just really confused, and you don't know how to move forward, then just take some time. You don't have to be in a hurry with the divorce."

"Maybe not," she agreed, "but it just seemed as if it would be so much easier."

"*Easier* is an interesting word," he stated thoughtfully. "I don't quite understand it from my viewpoint, but I get that, for you, maybe it eliminated one problem. And listen, if I am a problem, the divorce is exactly where you need to go because that's not what I'm here for. And, yes, it would have been nice if you had turned to me for help instead of seeing me as a problem."

"And that's exactly what I should have done," she confirmed. "I'm not even sure why I didn't."

"Maybe that answer will come to you when you think about it," he offered. "Right now, if you can get some sleep, I think you should."

They rang off soon afterward. She sat here on a park bench, thinking about it, not even sure of the answers to the questions he had posed.

When she got home, Kelly wheeled herself out, then looked at her and spat, "Looks as if you went out with lover boy again."

She frowned at that and then shook her head. "No, I didn't. I called him, was talking to him, however, trying to figure out what I'm doing with my life."

Her eyebrows shot up in a scowl. "Don't tell me that you're thinking about going back to him?" she asked in a mocking tone.

Keisha stared at her sister. "I don't understand why you have to be so hateful about him."

"I don't *have* to be," she declared, waving her hands, "but it's a whole lot easier. I have absolutely no intention of ever being friends with him."

"And yet you didn't have any problem with him at first."

"Yes, … I did," she spat, chewing on her words. "I didn't want him around. You did. And, sure, I may have had something to do with helping you decide to get rid of him— not being friendly with him and reminding you of all his faults. Maybe I should have passed on that message about his dad, but he wasn't right for you then and isn't right for you now. So I don't know why you would hold it against me."

"Do you know what's right for me though?" she asked. Kelly eyed Keisha curiously. "Do you have any idea what I need or want for my life?"

"Yeah, and it's not him," she snapped.

"How much of that is because you're afraid of being alone, afraid of not having a home?"

Her sister glared at her, suddenly angry. "Oh, no. … No, no, no. You're not …" Kelly was spitting mad now. "You won't pull a stunt like that with me."

"Oh, and what stunt is that?" Keisha asked, staring at her sister. "Because you're right. I did let you sway my decision. I did let all the times you ended up in hospital influence me, and that's why I told him that I needed space and time."

"And then you asked for the divorce."

"I did," she agreed, "and now I'm wondering if it was me wanting a divorce or if it was you telling me that I needed to divorce my husband."

Kelly laughed. "It probably was me telling you, but the fact that I could even tell you that"—she smirked—"says an awful lot about you, and the fact that you really didn't want him in your life. If you actually loved the man, nobody could tell you that." And, with that, she wheeled herself back out of the living room, laughing like a loon.

Keisha stared out in the distance. Kelly was right about that, if nothing else. But when it's been a long time, with issues of long distance, you get worn down and don't know where you're going and what you're doing. And suddenly you're listening to the wrong voices and the wrong people are telling you what to do.

In a way, Keisha hadn't made her own decision at all. She had just made the one that Kelly wanted her to make because her sister was so worried about being alone and being afraid. It wasn't Keisha's own decision at all, and that's where she had gone wrong.

Going up to her room, she brought out a journal and just started letting the emotions flow. She still had a long way to go, but she wasn't sure that divorcing Jaxon was the issue. Every time she thought about those divorce papers, her stomach twisted up in knots, and she realized just how much she didn't want the divorce. Then she would think about all the problems they'd had when he was here and realized she just couldn't live that way. But then again, they didn't have to. She didn't know what the solution was, but it didn't have to be that way, and, considering Kelly's attitude, a different solution would probably be better for Keisha as well as for him.

If he had such a tough time being here in the first place, who's to say he even wanted to come back anyway?

She wouldn't want to, not if it had been made so obvious that she wasn't welcome in the first place. And it wasn't just Kelly. Keisha herself hadn't made Jaxon feel welcome either. She should have been absolutely thrilled to see him but had very quickly let her sister's poisonous voice hit her in all the wrong places, and that's where everything went south.

Sad and ashamed of herself, Keisha worked her way through as much as she could by writing it down in her journal and then phoned her therapist and left a message, hoping for an appointment. The next day she went through the motions at work and knew her staff was looking at her sideways throughout the day. She tried hard to be what they needed and knew that she needed to kick this as fast as possible, but it was damn hard when she was stuck on some of the most basic issues.

When she walked in to her therapist's lobby later that day, he came to get her, a frown on his face, and walked her back to his private office.

"Your message sounded pretty serious."

She stared at him and nodded. "In a way, it is serious. And, in another way, it's been a long time coming."

Dr. Raul looked at her and nodded. "Then let's begin."

When her appointment was over, she sat outside in her car for a long moment. A lot had been shared. A lot had been brought up and had shown her even more issues that she didn't want to look at. Dr. Raul had been the first to say that she needed to go easy on this and that she shouldn't blame herself, reminding her that nothing was so far gone that she couldn't save it—if she really wanted to.

Exhausted to the point of no return, she fell asleep early. She woke up in the night with her phone ringing. She grabbed it and answered it, her voice sleepy.

"If you go back to him, you'll be sorry." And, with that, her caller disconnected.

It was that same mechanical voice that had been plaguing her for what seemed like an eternity. She stared down at the phone, shocked because it had to be somebody who actually knew who she was. What did they mean, saying she would be sorry? It sounded much more like a threat than an observation. When her phone rang again, she stared at it as if it was a viper about to explode, but she recognized the number as Jaxon's. "Hello?"

"You're awake?"

"Yeah, I just got one of those nasty phone calls."

He hesitated and then said, "So did I."

"Why is somebody doing that to us?" she cried out.

"What did yours say?"

She stopped, winced, and took a deep breath. "*If I go back to you, I'll be sorry,*" she repeated, quoting the voice on the phone.

"Yeah," he replied. "I got something pretty similar. More like, *If I go back, I'll be sorry.*"

"Somebody really doesn't want us to be together," she

noted, with a bad attempt at humor.

He didn't respond.

She continued. "I don't know who it is, and I don't have a clue why anybody would care. It's our life. Nobody else should have any issue with us."

"Oh, I agree," he confirmed, "but these calls are getting particularly … nasty."

"I think this is the first one that seems threatening," she noted. "I just don't know who cares enough."

"Yeah, maybe that's the question. Is your business in jeopardy?"

"What do you mean?"

"If we do get back together again, does it affect anything at the clinic?"

"Oh my," she replied, gasping and breathing heavily.

"Take a deep breath and calm down."

She took a couple deep breaths. "No, … not at all. It's been my practice and my business all along. It's always been my plan, and our marital status won't change anything."

"So, nobody will lose their job? You won't have to lay off anybody? Nobody has any fears along those lines?"

"I don't think so, and I don't know why they would," she replied immediately.

"It's certainly interesting," he noted. "I almost didn't call you, since it's late, but then I figured maybe you had gotten a call too."

"Yeah, I sure did," she noted, "but this one has unnerved me. There was more force, more anger, more something behind it."

"Yeah, I agree. So, you can't think of anybody else who might be against you being … I want to say, *being happy*, but I don't know if that's part of this."

"I don't know anybody who would do this," she stated.

"I don't either," he agreed. "Completely unrelated but we have an injured armadillo here. Timber calls him Pako."

"An armadillo?" she asked in astonishment. "What happened to him?"

"Looks as if he got into an argument with something, though I wouldn't have thought anything would pick a fight with him."

"Not often," she noted cautiously. "Do I need to come see him?"

"I, … I could either bring him to you or have you come here."

"It wouldn't hurt to check on the llamas too," she suggested, "and tomorrow is a half day anyway at the clinic. So maybe I'll come out in the afternoon."

"Okay, that sounds great. Look. I know it's an odd question, but the accident that killed your parents and injured Kelly, was anybody else involved?"

She stared down at her phone. "I don't know why you're asking that," she began, "but, yes, another vehicle was involved—two other vehicles actually. Some other cars got bumped, but I guess they classified it as a head-on collision. The other driver died too."

"Interesting," he muttered.

"I don't have too many of the details. I was so busy looking after Kelly and trying to bury my parents that finding out who the other driver was wasn't among my immediate needs at the time," she shared. "That's another ball I dropped and feel guilty about."

"Don't bother," he stated. "It's been a lot of years now."

"It has, but Kelly might benefit somehow if I'd gone in that direction. God, I hadn't really thought of it."

"I'm worried about it now. It just occurred to me that maybe the one thing somebody doesn't want is for you to be happy, and that would be someone who is unhappy themselves and who blames you."

"I don't know how anybody would think blaming me for their unhappiness would solve anything," she replied, "but it doesn't really make sense that it would involve that accident since I wasn't even there. I was finishing exams."

"Right," he muttered. "You weren't even in town then, were you?"

"No, I was at college," she stated. "I finished my last exam that day at three o'clock, then stepped outside and started to *whoop* and holler because I'd finally completed my studies. Then I got the phone call which basically ended everything I knew in my life."

"Interesting," he repeated, with a sigh.

"That's too many *interesting* comments coming out of you today."

"I'm sorry. That was really crappy timing. It's just that … my mind is spinning."

"Yes, crappy timing, yet, if it hadn't happened that way, I don't know if I would have been able to finish. Things were financially very tight for quite a while, and even now I'm still just trying to get back on my feet."

"And I was gone for quite a while."

"Yes, you were," she said, but this time she could see it for what it was—and the humor of it. "And apparently I just blocked all that out and went to work, not thinking about what you might need from me either."

"That part isn't of any importance at the moment," he told her, "but I really would like to get these phone calls to stop."

"You and me both." She groaned. "It just seems as if somebody hates me, and I don't know why."

"Has your sister gotten any calls like that?"

"I don't think so, but I can ask her."

"Might be a good idea," he suggested, "and, since you've hidden it from her, maybe she's been hiding something similar from you."

"Maybe," she murmured. "Anyway, I'll come out tomorrow afternoon."

"Okay, but talk to Kelly in the meantime." With that, he disconnected.

CHAPTER 15

THE FOLLOWING AFTERNOON Jaxon worked hard but kept an eye out for vehicles coming and going, knowing that Keisha would be here at some point. The other guys razzed him about it. He shrugged. "Hey, she's my wife. What was I supposed to do?" he asked, grinning like a fool. "Obviously I want a relationship with her, but, if not, I still want to maintain some sort of friendship."

"I don't know if you can be friends after a divorce," Tommy said, looking over at him. "It doesn't seem doable."

"I'm hoping we don't have to find a way to make it doable," Jaxon replied. "I know a lot of people can co-parent with a certain amount of ease afterward, but we aren't in that position."

"It sounds as if the sister might need co-parenting though," Tommy quipped, with a laugh.

"Yeah, and, if she heard that, she wouldn't appreciate it."

"No, I'm sure she wouldn't. It doesn't change the fact that, as much as Kelly's been dealt a tough hand in her life, it's also a tough hand for Keisha."

Jaxon couldn't argue with that. When her vehicle drove in, he felt such a sense of relief that it was palpable. He walked over and smiled as she got out. "Hey," he greeted her.

"Hey, so where is this Pako?" she asked, straight to the point. She was here for the armadillo, but it didn't make him feel any less happy that she came.

"She's over in the treatment center."

"She?" she asked, with a chuckle.

"Honest to God, I couldn't tell, and I didn't want to take a closer look."

"Why?"

"They're more exotic animals."

"Exotic and domestic," she clarified. "I did an exotic specialty, just because so few people handle those kinds of animals. I thought it might give a little extra boost to my practice."

"Did it help?"

"Yeah, … absolutely. A lot of my clients have exotic pets—lots of snakes," she noted, with a smile. "Then you get your fair share of weasels and other critters. Plus, we do a certain amount of wildlife rescue work. A lot of the rescue organizations bring their animals to me, or I go to them, if needed."

"Hard to imagine," he noted, with half a smile.

She looked over at him and nodded. "Might be hard to imagine, yet it's a decision I'm quite happy with."

"That's all that matters," he replied immediately.

She shrugged. "It's definitely been a help in terms of keeping the business afloat, especially in the beginning."

As they entered the treatment center, she walked over as he brought out a rather large cage. She looked at the armadillo and frowned. "Definitely not on the happy side, is she?" She took the animal out of the cage and, with gloves on, carefully checked it over. It was definitely a female, so Pako was not an inept name. She'd only worked with a couple of armadillos in the past, and this one was definitely struggling with something. It took her a few minutes to sort it out.

Then she frowned.

"She's obviously dehydrated and suffering," she shared. "One foot is injured, but I'm not seeing anything else that is major." She stroked the animal's head. "If her foot's painful though, she may not have been able to forage."

"It's a she?" Jaxon asked.

"It's definitely a she and potentially pregnant." He eyed Keisha in astonishment. "An armadillo pregnancy," she noted, with a laugh, "is rather unique as it is."

"How is that?"

"They can choose when to get pregnant after a couple years. Once the decision is made, they will then have four babies, always four babies," she stated, with a smile. "One egg splits in two, and then each of the two eggs split again."

He shook his head at that. "Always?"

"Mother Nature is like that."

"Yeah, tell me about it." He laughed.

"She runs like clockwork, and, as long as you're on her clock, she's fine. It's when things go wrong that issues happen," she added, with a smile. She checked out the leg, and Pako gave her very little trouble, mostly staying as curled up as she could, except for the part of the leg that Keisha held.

Jaxon noted, "She doesn't seem to be fighting you too much."

"No, she isn't," she confirmed. "I'm hoping it's because she realizes I'm here to help."

Just then Tiffany walked in, saw what they were doing, and joined them. "May I help?" she asked.

Keisha smiled. "I think this leg will heal on its own. I also think she's pregnant, and something steered her away from her home." She looked back at Jaxon. "Any idea where she came from?"

"Pretty close," he replied. "I can take her back there."

"That would be good. She is quite likely nesting."

"In that case let's go." He opened up the crate, and Keisha put the little female inside and looked over at Tiffany. "You want to come?"

"Yeah," she said immediately. "I would love to. Can't say I've ever worked on an armadillo."

"I've only worked on four, but they are cool and one of the unique animals in the world," Keisha shared, with a smile. "Let's see if we can take her back to her place and release her."

And that's what they did. They took horses out to keep the noise and disruption down as much as they could. Danny the donkey didn't appreciate being left behind and brayed louder with every step they took away from him. When they got to the area where they first found Pako, Keisha hopped off the horse and walked around, looking for a potential burrow. It didn't take her long, and she motioned with her hand.

Jaxon came over with the crate and set it down beside her.

She pointed at the burrow. "I can't be sure it's Pako's by any means, but this would be a typical armadillo burrow."

He opened up the crate and shifted it enough that Pako slid toward the door.

Keisha smiled and nodded. "Now, if we just leave her be, there's a good chance she'll find her own way from here. Let's just back up and see what she does."

And they all stepped back and watched. Suddenly Pako uncurled, sniffed the air around her, and moved into the nearby burrow.

"Do you think she'll stay there now?" Jaxon asked.

"I can't be certain," Keisha admitted. "She may decide it's not safe, but I would certainly avoid coming here for the next little while, if you can."

"You don't think we need to check up on her?" Tiffany asked.

"No, I'm presuming that whatever happened to her was something she recovered from on her own, but she may have just been shocked. I don't even know what to say, but the leg had healed quite nicely on its own at this point."

"Good enough for me," Jaxon replied. "I just wanted to confirm she was okay. She wasn't moving, even after the dogs had surrounded her."

"Which is also her mechanism for how to save herself," Keisha explained, turning to him. "You can come by and check up on her. Just don't go close to the burrow."

"I won't." With a last backward glance, they moved out, and they all headed back to the main cabin.

∩

WITH TIFFANY LEADING the way, Keisha asked, "How are the llamas?"

"That's next," Tiffany said, with a smile. "Yet, when I heard you were here, I wanted to come take a look."

"Now let's go check on the llamas together."

They spent the next three hours working with the llamas, checking temperatures, checking feet, checking weights, and recording all the data. When they had been through all the llamas, Keisha nodded. "I think these guys are doing great. They'll need a few months to pick up some weight and to adjust to the new location, but they are settling in nicely."

"They should be," Timber declared, as he came up behind them. "They're getting the best of everything." No rancor was in his tone. He was truly happy to help.

Keisha smiled at him. "You're doing a good thing here."

"You might think that doing a good thing would give you kudos in this life," Timber noted, with a chuckle. "Happily, I'm not doing it for that reason. Still, every once in a while, I need to bring in extra money. It would sure be nice if people saw rescues as a valid enterprise, worthy of generosity."

"Don't they contribute?" Jaxon asked. "I would have thought all kinds of animal lovers were around here."

"No, not so much. It's not that the locals aren't animal lovers, but I get some who think that I should be helping the homeless or the veterans or single mothers or at-risk youth," he shared. "And I agree. There should be help for everybody. The thing is, not all of us can contribute to every worthy project. However, I do think that, if enough of us follow our hearts and give what we can where we choose to help, everybody should more or less be covered—in theory. So, I try to look after the animals. That's my niche. So I don't want animals falling through the cracks, and, with the tough times right now, we're getting an awful lot of animals dropped off."

Keisha glanced at Jaxon, seeing how happy and content he looked out here. The Haven was as much here for him as for these animals.

"We have two more horses coming in today." Timber shared, with a smile.

"Really?" Tiffany asked. "Surrenders?"

"Yes, the details just came in. They just can't keep the animals anymore, but they are bringing over what they have left for feed and grain," Timber noted. "I've agreed to take them, but I'm also aware that I've got to keep the numbers of animals we take in under control."

Jaxon looked at him and smiled. "And that'll never happen, if it means you have to turn them away," he stated flatly. "I know you too well."

"Yet there has to be some limit on the numbers we take in," Timber stated. "Otherwise I'll get carried away with too much, too soon. I don't want to get into a position where I can't look after the ones I have."

"Of course not," Jaxon agreed, "but you also know that we're all here to help if we can."

"Sure, but just the cost of putting hay out for these guys over the winter if needed," he pointed out, with a wry look, "could be pretty rough."

"Of course, and again, if there's anything I can do to help, I'm in."

He smiled. "Come on, Jaxon. You're already working for free," he reminded him. "So I'm not sure anything else can be done."

Jaxon shrugged. "If free isn't cutting it, then maybe we need to get some jobs to help pay for this too."

Timber stared at him in shock and then shook his head. "No, that's not necessary. In theory, I'm fine moneywise for now. It's just that sometimes, when I think about the future, I cringe. We've already put out so much money on all these buildings and the treatment center." He cast a glance at Tiffany, who shrugged.

"It'll just take a little bit of time to recoup some of that from the contributions," she replied. "I haven't checked the GoFundMe page in a while, but that's a good reminder."

"I don't want to take out any more loans, for now at

least," Timber said, with a laugh. "So, it might have to be beans and rice for a while."

"I'm good with that," Jaxon confirmed cheerfully. "As long as I'm not sleeping in the bunkhouse."

At that, some of the other men nearby groaned. "Eating beans, sleeping in the bunkhouse? No way," they cried out.

Jaxon laughed at them. Keisha smiled, enjoying seeing him happy.

Timber shrugged. "Better than not having anything to eat."

"Yeah, it is, but beans for dinner and sharing a bunkhouse? No, no, no."

Dwight and Toby stood on the front porch, listening in, thinking about what Timber had just said. Dwight interjected, "I am not trying to be thick here, but I don't think things will be that bad. We've got a good store of foodstuffs. By the way, one of the feed distributors is looking to talk to you."

"What do they want?" he asked him.

"They're asking what kind of center you're setting up and wondering if they can help. I told them that we would appreciate all the help that we could get."

Timber smiled and nodded. "I'm not much of a people person, but these are definitely times when I can put on a smile and act gracious."

"Yep. This would be one of them. He wants you to give him a call."

"That's even better. I won't even have to get dressed up," Timber quipped. He took his leave and headed inside, and everyone else headed into the main part of the kitchen, looking for coffee.

Burke patted Jaxon on the back and said, "We can go over the work schedule tomorrow morning. Why don't you take the rest of the day off?" And, with a glance toward Keisha, he whispered, "Looks as if you might need a little bit of time."

"I was hoping to talk to Gregory, so Tommy first."

"Gregory?" Burke did a double-take. "Why do you need to talk to the whiz kid?"

Jaxon filled him in about the whole lot of it, since Burke had been away for the last few days.

Burke listened patiently to Jaxon's and Keisha's newest set of problems, then asked a few questions of his own. He added, "Gregory is a good one. With all the BS I dealt with from my ex, … he's been a godsend." And he launched into his story involving his ex-girlfriend, Silvia—who also happened to be the sister of Shirley, Burke's current girl-friend. Silvia stole his identity via his three credit card accounts, living on his credit with her con-artist boyfriend, Frankie. Gregory helped them compile the data, file the reports, and eventually proved that Burke had done nothing to max out his credit lines. Burke frowned at Jaxon and asked, "So where did Gregory get to in your particular case?"

"I haven't heard anything yet, so don't know how far he's gotten. He's a busy guy though, I hear. I didn't want to bother him yet."

"I hear you," Burke noted, "but you may want to sort it out before it gets out of hand."

Jaxon nodded. "Keisha and I are both getting some pret-ty ugly phone calls now."

At that, everybody turned to face him, staring between Keisha and him. "What do you mean by ugly phone calls?" Burke asked, as he turned to Keisha.

Keisha explained about the one she got in the middle of the night. "This is the first one that felt like a direct threat," she noted, "but the whole thing is out of hand."

"Of course it is," Burke agreed.

EVERYBODY STARTED TO talk, and, by the end of it, Jaxon walked over to Timber, who had just come back inside and stood at the kitchen counter, shoving cookies in his mouth. "I need a favor," Jaxon said in a low tone.

"Ask away," Timber replied, sliding the cookie jar over in front of Jaxon.

"Do you know anybody who could pull up some information on an accident?"

Timber froze and frowned at him. "What's going on, Jaxon?"

He told him about the car accident that killed Keisha's parents and injured her sister. "I just wondered if these calls could be related to that."

"It seems to be a good avenue to check out at least," Timber agreed.

"It does, but I'm not exactly sure where to start."

"We've got a friendly detective in town," Timber pointed out. "He's bailed us out a couple times already. Give Richard Martin a call. He should be able to give you the details."

"He won't have any issues handing out confidential information?"

"It shouldn't be a problem, particularly since it involved Keisha's family. Besides, Richard is ex-military too, so he's one of us," Timber explained and left it at that.

"Right, Keisha is one of the surviving family members, so maybe it wouldn't be a problem anyway."

"Did you ask her about it?"

"I did, and she doesn't remember a whole lot of the details. She never even requested a copy of the accident report or anything else. Part of the problem is that, in her mind, it was just a terrible accident. I don't know if fault was determined or not, but the driver of the other vehicle—deemed to have hit her family head-on—was also killed."

"Ah." Timber nodded, with an understanding look. "In that case, that would be a potential avenue for finding people who are unhappy."

"Exactly. I just thought maybe it was a line to tug."

With that, Timber nodded, then pulled out his phone and wrote down Richard's number. "I highly suggest you go give that particular line a hard pull."

CHAPTER 16

THE NEXT COUPLE days followed the same pattern. Keisha went to the clinic, worked herself to the bone, came home, and made dinner for her and Kelly. She spoke to Jaxon every evening, checking in to see how his day had gone.

Kelly ignored Keisha almost completely, but the leftovers disappeared during the day, so at least she was eating at some point in time. Unsure how to make her any happier, Keisha realized she could do only so much. Kelly did have to want to help herself for any other assistance to take hold. Being left in a wheelchair was an awful lot to be dealt with in Kelly's life, and Keisha didn't know how to help her, other than giving her a place to live and food and as much emotional support as Kelly would accept—which was none at all. At some point in time, her sister would need more help than Keisha could give her, but that was a conversation she really didn't want to have. Not to mention the fact that Kelly wasn't currently open to any conversation at all.

As Keisha went through the next couple days, she got one more disturbing phone call and then none. She was grateful for that, yet it worried her, and she mentioned it to Jaxon that night.

He shared, "I went to see a local detective whom Timber knows, asking about any relevant information in the case file on the accident that killed your parents."

She froze and then asked, "Why would you do that?" She was more puzzled than anything.

"Because the other driver also died," he stated, "and that would be a good reason for somebody in his family to be very angry that you are living your life, while their loved one isn't."

"Yeah, but I'm not exactly thriving," she clarified, then hesitated. "Yet you're right. If I was killed in the accident, it would be a completely different story."

"And we also know that unhappy people don't think things through rationally," he pointed out. "Plus, we are getting all these strange phone calls. I did tell Richard about them, and he should get around to calling you at some point to get your statement as well. Meanwhile, Gregory, the digital PI guy, said that he couldn't trace the calls to my phone, probably made with disposable phones being used once and thrown away. Regardless, it's definitely something that needs to be checked out. You are getting threats. I am getting threats. So we'll see what Richard can find. We both need someone to figure out what is what."

"I know. I understand," she replied. "I'm hardly even answering my phone because of it. I do have a work phone, but it's separate."

"Good, so just maintain that setup. ... Did you talk to Kelly about it?"

"No, she hasn't been talking to me at all," she noted. "Honest to God, I don't know what to do with her."

"That's another completely different issue," he stated. "You may need to talk to her about that accident too."

Keisha gave a broken laugh. "I don't know what the hell is going on, but, whatever it is, my sister is heading into a tailspin again."

He asked, "Does she know that you and I are talking?"

"Yes, she does." She waited through the pause on his end, knowing what was coming. So, before he could say anything, she added, "And, no, I don't know if it's because of that."

"Right, well, … at least we're both aware of the possibility."

"Yeah," she said, bitterness in her tone. "I just don't want to even contemplate that she thinks it'll have an impact on us getting to know each other."

"But it did have an impact last time," he pointed out.

"You're right." Keisha sighed. "I don't know what to say."

"For the moment, there's nothing to say. We'll just continue as we are."

"Do you think it's the right thing to do?"

"Yes, I do. I'm not willing to give you up without a fight." And, with that, he disconnected.

She stared down at the phone and realized that really was what it all came down to. She had been avoiding the question, about whether or not she loved him, whether or not she wanted him over everything else, but the answer was very clear in her heart. She absolutely loved him.

Otherwise she wouldn't be doing what she was doing.

The trouble was, her sister wasn't making it easy, and she could see that, for Kelly, this would likely be some major trauma about losing Keisha, on top of the losses Kelly had already endured—her parents and her own mobility. But, dammit, Keisha was entitled to a life as well. That was easy enough to say in her mind, … until she was forced to deal with Kelly's trauma over and over again, plus Kelly's ways of gaining attention so Keisha would never leave her. It was a really messed-up scenario—one she didn't want to deal with at all.

When she came back from walking the dogs the following evening, Kelly was in the kitchen, looking for food.

"The leftovers are on the stove," Keisha said.

Her sister didn't say anything and just continued to rummage.

"I guess I might as well stop cooking then, if you're not eating."

Kelly shrugged. "Can't say that you're cooking anything I like."

She stared at her. "Everything I'm cooking is food you have always eaten."

"I'm not eating them now," she snapped, as she shut the refrigerator door, turned, and glared at her, fire in her eyes. "So, how long before you kick me out?"

Keisha stared at her in shock for a moment. "Why would …" she stammered, then took a deep breath. "Why would I do that?" she asked, looking at Kelly closely, seeing the tears, the fear, and so much else.

"It's obvious that you're spending all your spare time with him now."

"Jaxon is my husband, Kel," she reminded her sister.

"Whatever that means," Kelly muttered, trying to hold back the tears, but one slipped down, which she rubbed away. "You're trying to divorce him, remember? You were pretty-damn quick to get rid of him before."

She stared at Kelly and felt the shame wash over her. "Yes, I was," she agreed, "and that is something I'll have to live with for the rest of my life."

Kelly looked at her in surprise. "What do you mean?"

"It was the wrong thing to do," she declared. "I just couldn't handle the stress between the two of you, and I took the easy way out."

"Right, so what now? You got rid of him, but now that ... kicking him out didn't seem to work out, so you'll get rid of me?" She spat out her words, then sat here chewing her lips bloody. "Is that it?" she snapped.

"No, it isn't, but honestly, I'm not at all sure what to do with you."

"You don't need to do anything with me," she snapped again. "I'm not a child."

"You sure are acting like one. I cook a meal, and you won't show up. I talk to you, and you roll away. There's absolutely no point in having any discussion with you because you won't do anything beyond hurling the insults at me and at Jaxon."

Her sister stared at her. "I don't understand why he has to be in our lives."

"I know you don't," Keisha replied, calm and collected. "However, I love him and always have. I want him in my life."

"You don't even know him," Kelly shrieked. "He came back a complete stranger. Those are not my words. You're the one who said that."

"You know what? Right about now, *you* are the complete stranger," Keisha pointed out, trying so hard not to snap, but Kelly was impossible. "I allowed you to affect my decision before, and it was wrong. I wasn't fair to him at all. He had come back with just as much trauma as you're living with, and, instead of being there for him, as a loving wife should"—she gave a dry laugh—"I was all about you. You are the one who put me in a position of having to choose between the two of you, and that was wrong. I shouldn't have to make a choice. There shouldn't have been a choice to make. There's absolutely no reason the two of you can't get along."

"I'm not getting along with him," Kelly declared, staring at her sister. "So that's off the table."

"Okay. That's off the table, and you are allowed to have your opinions. Just tell me this. … What will you do with your life?" she asked, hardly pulling back her tone. When Kelly just shrugged, Keisha's own anger surged. "What will you do, Kel? Run away and hide every time he shows up? Just disappear and not have any communication with anybody in this world?"

Kelly now stared at her, open-mouthed, not used to the pushback.

"I know that being in a wheelchair is so unfair, and I get that. I know it's hard and full of challenges, but I can't change that. So, if the doctors can't help you, I don't know who can, except for maybe a therapist."

"I won't go to therapy," she muttered, her voice unnaturally calm. "And you can't make me."

"No, I can't make you, but I'm also not sure what to do with you. You aren't making the slightest effort to get along with anybody," Keisha explained. "It used to be just other people you shouted at and insulted, and now … it's me. You're not making it easier on any of us."

"Of course it's you," she replied in the same neutral tone. "You've made a decision, and, if you're not for me, you're against me, and you've made that quite clear."

She stared at her in shock. "I have not. At no point in time have I ever done that—"

"Yes, you have," Kelly interrupted, "and, for the record,

I don't want anything to do with you either."

"So, what then? You'll just live here in silence?" she asked. "You've accused me of doing something horrible and won't give me any explanation as to how you came to that repugnant answer. You won't even talk to me."

"No, I won't talk to you," she stated, with a dismissive wave of her hand. "You made your decision, so that's all there is to it." With that, she turned and wheeled her way out.

However, this time Keisha circled around and stood in the doorway. "No, and that's enough of that, Kel. You don't get to throw accusations at me, then turn and roll away like you always do. That is no way for us to have a discussion."

"I don't want to discuss anything with you."

"No, you don't, and that's because you don't want to be called out for acting like a child. You just don't want me to have a life. You're miserable and have decided that I must be miserable too. I'm sorry that I can't give you the life you had. You did have everything here with Mom, even after Dad got sick. I don't know anything about what happened in the accident, but I have done my darndest to make a decent life for you since it happened, and honestly, you don't appreciate it. I don't think you really give a crap one way or the other. There is funding for you to get surgery if you need it, and there is money for retraining. There is money for all kinds of stuff to get you set up and moving forward, but you don't seem to care. You apparently don't want to move forward with your life at all."

"Why would I?" she bellowed. "This"—she waved at her wheelchair—"this is my life, and nobody wants to live this way."

"No, nobody wants it, but they aren't determined to

make everybody else pay."

Kelly gasped. "You mean, for my mistakes? Is that what you were going to say?"

Keisha stood here in astonishment. For few moments, she was unable to speak at all. "No, Kel, I had no intention of saying anything of the kind and never would. I don't know what mistakes you're even talking about."

Her sister snapped her jaw shut. "That's a damn good thing," she muttered, then tried to leave the room.

As she tried to get around Keisha, who still stood in the doorway, she banged into the wall, then in absolute frustration, she hit it with a fury that surprised both of them, back-and-forth, back-and-forth, until her shoulders started to shake, and tears formed in her eyes. Then finally her sister backed up one more time and tore out of the kitchen, making her way past the wall.

Keisha was left stunned and in tears herself, as she watched her sister. Keisha didn't know how to help Kelly or what Keisha was supposed to do about this, if anything. It all just seemed to be way beyond her. How was she supposed to give her sister any kind of support when Kelly didn't want anything? Yet she still wanted everything.

The next morning, she made coffee and stepped out on the deck, where she phoned Kelly's counselor and admitted, "I don't know how to handle her anymore."

"Tell me what's going on."

And, for the next twenty minutes, she dumped all the things that her sister was doing to make her life so difficult.

"She needs to come in and talk to me, for one," the therapist suggested.

"Yeah, I've mentioned that, but she refuses to go to therapy. There doesn't seem to be anything I can do, but she's determined that I shouldn't have my marriage. She feels that I chose him over her and that there is absolutely no way she will move forward in life because of the wheelchair."

"That's because she hasn't fully accepted where she is right now," Adam noted.

"And she's still not interested in accepting the reality of her life," Keisha confirmed, frustrated as ever. "Adam, she's still so angry, and yet she mentioned something about *her fault*, and I don't know what that was all about."

He went silent for a moment. "I don't know either," he murmured, "unless it has to do with the fact that your parents passed away and that she couldn't do anything to save them."

Keisha immediately felt terrible about her own feelings and groaned. "That could be it. I just don't know how to deal with her and haven't really dealt with my own grief because of it."

"It's a never-ending cycle," Adam murmured. "See if you can get her to talk to me. I do house calls, but it's likely to be a waste of time if she won't let me in or won't open up to me."

"I know, but how am I supposed to deal with it? I can see that I let her sabotage my relationship with my husband already in the past," she shared, "and I'm not willing to do that anymore."

"Good," Adam agreed, "because you can't just be her caretaker. That is not your only role in life. It isn't who she would want you to be either, but she's not capable of seeing past where she is right now," he shared, his voice calm and sympathetic. "She does need to get some help though."

"I know, and I'm afraid that she's making herself sick too—not eating, falling, ramming her wheelchair into the wall," Keisha added. "It just feels as if she's doing anything she can to stop me from doing what I want to do. She succeeded at that once, and the reality of me going back to Jaxon now has sent her around the bend."

"And her reaction makes sense, but it's not the answer to her problems—or yours. You get to have a life too," he stated, "and nobody gets to destroy their caretaker if they don't get what they want."

"If Kelly and I could get along and if she would be respectful to my husband, it would be a different story," Keisha noted. "Jaxon won't mind. Hell, he would be first to support her because he's experienced plenty of hell of his own."

"But Kelly's anger and hatred seems directly related to losing you?"

"Yes," she confirmed, "and that just makes me feel even guiltier."

"Which is also partly why she's doing it," Adam pointed out.

"So, what then? I'm supposed to just do … what? She won't go any place where she can get help. She won't go into a facility either—one where she could have other people around her who are in wheelchairs too—so she could learn to get past some of this."

"And it's not even so much that she needs that community," Adam shared. "She needs psychological help, but I don't know if that's anything you'll give her help with, in terms of adjusting to her new life."

"But it's been years, Adam," she said, "and she's still just not adjusting."

"No, because she's angry, and she doesn't want to adjust, but that's not your problem."

"And yet it feels very much as if it's my problem because she's making it my problem."

"Then you need to limit her ability to do that," Adam replied. "And, sure, it'll feel as if you're deserting Kelly, and we don't want you to feel guilty about that too, but she needs to come up with solutions for her own life, beyond just the anger that chases everybody away. And it's worth doing right now because, if her ploy didn't work to chase away your husband, and you've chosen to go back to him, effectively choosing him over her, she will get even more depressed." He hesitated and asked, "How bad is her mental state?"

"I don't know," she admitted, frustration evident in her tone. "She won't talk to me. Kelly is just this black pit of anger."

"I'm sorry," he murmured. "That just makes life even harder on you."

"It does, and that's not even the problem, as much as not knowing how to deal with it going forward."

He didn't say anything for a moment and then offered, "Look. How about if I stop by tomorrow afternoon and see how she handles it?"

"Thank you," she muttered. "I would appreciate that very much." And, with that, she ended the call and sat here for the longest time.

When Kelly wheeled past, Keisha realized that her sister had been sitting around the corner, undoubtedly listening to Keisha's phone call with Adam. She called out her sister over it. "If you don't want to hear things that you won't like, you shouldn't be lurking around while I make private phone calls."

Her sister was silent, then came almost a growl, as if to

say, *If I had somebody to love me, I wouldn't be in this situation.*

Keisha froze for a moment, then moved inside, staring at her sister, who was now wheeling herself toward her own bedroom. "So, is all this because you think I don't love you or because you don't have a partner? I never even considered that maybe you were jealous."

"I'm not jealous," Kelly snapped.

As Keisha studied her sister, she realized it was very likely the answer. "But you do assume that you'll never get a partner yourself, right?"

She turned and looked at her, an odd expression on her face. "Do you see anybody lining up?" she asked in a mocking tone. "Nobody wants to be with a paraplegic."

"I'm not so sure about that," Keisha countered, staring at her sister. "But far more problematic than your physical condition is your mental attitude, especially the anger that you keep spitting out on everybody."

Kelly laughed. "You have no idea how I feel."

"No, I don't because you're *always* so angry, and you won't even talk to me. It didn't use to be this way, Kel."

"Sure, but now I've realized that you're not really my sister anymore."

"What are you talking about?" she asked in exasperation.

"You're just … his wife."

And she spat that answer out with such force that Keisha was shocked. "You hate him that much?" she asked, unable to believe that her sister would literally view it that way.

Her sister stared at her and shrugged. "I don't particularly hate *him*. He's just a man, but I do hate what he represents."

"And what is that?"

"Progress in your life," she declared, her gaze fiery. "Progress in your life, … when I have absolutely no hope of making any progress in mine."

CHAPTER 17

JAXON STEPPED INTO Richard's office and took the seat he was offered.

Richard asked, "So, what is your interest in this case?" He tapped the file in front of him. "Other than the obvious connection, since it involved your wife's family."

"The question really has more to do with Keisha's sister, Kelly, who was badly injured in the accident," he clarified, "and the fact that Keisha and I have both been getting some pretty ugly, and now threatening, phone calls."

Detective Richard Martin's eyebrows went up. "You did mention something about that on the phone."

He nodded. "I did, and I'm hoping that I might find something relevant in the accident case file."

He frowned at that. "What makes you think anything would be here?"

"Because I don't know who else would be so against Keisha moving on and being happy, unless somebody out there thinks she doesn't deserve to live, like the other driver didn't survive."

"Meaning that somebody related to this case could potentially have that as a serious thought, since Keisha is living her life, and somebody out there resents it?"

"Something like that, yeah. Keisha wasn't even in town when it happened," he told Richard. "She was finishing off her college exams and had just written her final one and was prepared to go celebrate with her friends after all those years of hard work to become a veterinarian. Instead she got a phone call saying her parents had died in a car accident, and her sister was severely injured."

Richard winced at that. "Talk about life-changing information."

"Exactly, and her sister is still so angry and still not dealing at all with her situation as a paraplegic," he added, with a headshake. "As a veteran, I am well aware of things that she could do to help her situation, but she isn't interested, just wants to vent her anger on everyone around her."

"And that's always hard because nobody can make Kelly move forward if she herself is not ready to move forward."

"Exactly, and I get that. Believe me that she's not only *not* ready to move forward but she hates absolutely everything about me. Whether that's jealousy in the sense that Keisha will have a life, I don't know," he said. "There are no good answers in Kelly's mind."

Richard stared at him for a long moment, then nodded. "Opening this door could bring up a lot more pain for everybody. You know that, right?"

"I was hoping all the information wouldn't need to come out in the open," he stated. "I just wanted to see if any connections would make sense, as far as these threatening computerized phone calls go. Remember that both Keisha and I get them, almost in succession with each set of calls."

"Since we don't have any details on these calls yet," he pointed out, "I can't even give you any answers."

"Right. They come up as Private Numbers, and they're pretty consistently sent, received in tandem, both her and me."

"Meaning?"

"Meaning, that they are a lot more frequent than they were, … and both of us are getting hit, so the two of us are being targeted. If I get a call, I phone her and find out she just got one too."

"Does anybody know about your divorce—or pending divorce?" he asked, using his words carefully.

"No, and now that the two of us are talking again, I'm hopeful that the divorce won't happen," he shared. "That would be news to anybody."

"Interesting," he murmured. "You would think that the phone calls would go to the sister, Kelly, since she survived."

"Yeah, but maybe they feel as if Kelly has been punished enough."

"Ah," he noted, as he stared at him. "That makes a certain amount of sense."

"Maybe, I don't know. I'm just trying to figure it out myself. I have asked Keisha to talk to Kelly and see if she is getting these phone calls, but she is not being very forthcoming about anything at this point. Plus, Kelly used to warn her all the time about putting personal information out on the internet, and Keisha thinks somewhere along the line that she must have, since someone got her number. I, on the other hand, have never done anything with social media nor posted things on the internet at all," he explained. "So I have no idea where my phone number would have been found."

"It could have come from a completely different source," Richard suggested. "Just because you both assume it was info on social media, that doesn't mean it was."

Jaxon shrugged. "I'm sure people have their way of getting phone numbers. I just don't know what that is. It's not what I did in the military, so I'm a little behind the times technologically."

"What did you do?"

"Logistics. This last deployment, I was part of the maintenance crew," he replied. "I've certainly done my share of covert missions and all, but I'm also a carpenter, cabinet-maker, or whatever you want to call it. So, I was part of an advance team that would go out early and set up the camps. Then I'm there to fix things and to keep things moving the way they're supposed to," he added, with half a smile.

"So, how did you get injured?"

"Friendly fire," he stated, his tone curt.

"And you don't think that has anything to do with it?"

"No, I don't think so," he stated, with a headshake. "It was an accident. Just a really shitty accident that sidelined me from the work I was doing, which I loved. If I'd been single, I probably would have stayed, but I had a marriage to come home to. One that I didn't realize was falling apart, and that's on me."

"No, it's not just on you," Richard argued. "You're not the first man to come home to chaos. It's at least partly because you're different, and they're different too. Time has gone by, and everyone isn't necessarily understanding about how much adjustment is required."

"I certainly didn't understand, and I'm not sure I even do now. It's been a rough time for us all," he shared. "When you think about it, that wasn't even in my thought process."

"Of course not," Richard agreed, with a nod.

They all knew of cases where military people had come home, only to find out they didn't even have relationships anymore, but that wasn't the case for Jaxon. The relationship had been there but had gotten really complicated because of Kelly. And that's what he told Richard.

"And the car accident?" Richard asked him.

"It was before my time. I guess I didn't handle it that well with Kelly initially. Of course, in the meantime, I'd also been to rehab and had seen the differences in how wounded people healed, and I saw how much that mental attitude could make the difference. I wasn't up for coddling Kelly either and didn't show a whole lot of patience," he conceded, "and that is on me."

Richard didn't say anything and looked down at his notes. "Is there a pattern to when you get these phone calls?"

"Not really, all day, all night, yet I do feel as if it's been a little more often in the evenings. At times we get them in the middle of the night even. Since I've been back, and we figured out that each of us was getting these harassing phone calls, we've determined that some happen within a few minutes of the other."

"Both of you?"

"Yes"—he nodded immediately—"both of us."

"Interesting," Richard muttered, "because you would think that would be a time frame that other people would be sleeping."

"Or maybe they want to confirm that we don't get a chance to sleep."

"Right, back to thinking it's something deliberate."

He stared at the detective. "How can it not be deliberate when it's phone calls to both of our phones, within minutes of getting a Private Number call? And with a very specific warning message about our marriage. That was a game changer for me."

Richard laughed. "Yeah, good point. So obviously you both are being targeted, and this is deliberate. What we don't know is why or by whom."

"I realize this kind of incident isn't a big-budget item for you guys, so there is potentially no interest in following up," Jaxon acknowledged, "but I did want to confirm that you knew about it—in case anything were to happen. I would also like to follow up myself, if I can."

Richard looked at him and asked, "And what exactly would you do?"

"I want to look at the names of all the people involved in this one accident. I understand at least three vehicles were involved. I want to see who passed on and who was left behind. All of that should be public record anyway," he pointed out.

"So, it's not as if I'm really doing anything for you by giving you this information."

"I know, but no charges were filed, right?"

"No, it was deemed an accident."

"Okay, so, if it was an accident, and there were no charges, I have to wonder if that had any effect on how this person may have recovered."

"Or *not* recovered, you mean?"

"Yeah, recovered, not recovered. However you want to look at it," he said, with a smile. "There could potentially be answers in the police report somewhere."

"If you say so. I'm not so sure about that, but I can understand that you might think so."

Jaxon stared at him. "I don't know what to think," he admitted. "I'm just working my way through things."

"Of course you are, same as we would."

"But the bottom line is that somebody is doing this, and, if I could at least understand their motivation," Jaxon explained, "I might be able to convince them to stop, but that would mean actually meeting them."

With that, Richard handed over the original police file he had pulled for him. "Here is the police report and the forensic information. Read it, take notes, whatever, but you can't take this with you. The incident was deemed an accident due to bad weather. I don't know if we'll ever know what happened, and I understand your sister-in-law doesn't necessarily remember what happened either."

He nodded. "Who was in the other car?"

"The other victim was an older man. There was no evidence of a heart attack or other medical condition, so there was no reason to believe it was caused by that," Richard shared, pointing to a picture. "Honestly, the scene was a huge mess by the time we got there. Other vehicles were off the road, and everybody was running all over the place, trying to get people out of vehicles and off to the hospital. In fact, Kelly might have been better off left in the vehicle, considering the damage to her spine," Richard noted, as he put a picture in front of Jaxon. "But the bystanders were trying to get her out of the vehicle because a fire had started."

Jaxon grimaced. "That's a common problem, both moving the injured and avoiding the car fires that erupt after these accidents. You can't even consider everything else that might have happened in a situation like that," he noted.

Richard nodded. "You just have to do the best you can, which is what everybody did, and the end result was that she's paralyzed, hates her life, and now nobody can do anything to help her make it better—including you. Yet, at some point, she has to decide how she wants to live the life she has now, and that does not mean making you and your wife miserable."

"Yeah, she doesn't see it that way yet." Jaxon sighed. "I

don't really want to upset the apple cart any further because I know all too well what happened last time."

Detective Richard nodded. "That makes sense, but that's all I've got for you."

Jaxon thanked the detective, then stood up and walked out of Richard's office. As he stepped out the door to Richard's office, his phone rang. Recognizing the Private Number on his screen, he turned back to Richard, who was speaking to someone, and said, "Looks like it's our caller now."

Richard immediately walked over and said, "Answer it, and put it on Speaker."

When he did, that same chilling and mocking laughter filled the room. Several of the other cops within earshot stopped and listened. Then the caller asked, "Do you think the cops will help?"

"What do you think?" Jaxon asked.

"Not one bit." And, with that, the call terminated.

Jaxon faced Richard. "So how the hell does he know that I'm here?"

Richard gave him an odd look. "That is a completely different story," he declared, staring at the phone. He asked for it immediately and said, "I'll take this to our techs and see if they can get anything from that call."

"Sure, but I've got to tell you, every time, … like every damn time, it's always a Private Number, and it's never long enough to get it traced."

"So, he's also savvy and—"

"Very vindictive," interjected one of the other cops, frowning at Richard. "I don't know what this is about, but I don't like the sound of that call."

"No, neither do I," Richard confirmed, as he scratched

his chin. "Give us a little bit, Jaxon. Just take a seat. If you need anything, you can talk to Paul here." With that, Richard took off with Jaxon's phone, having a handle on it.

Paul stared at Jaxon, shrugged, and went back to his work.

But, for Jaxon, all he could do was sit here and wait, and he couldn't even tell Timber what was going on. Timber had sent him into town to do this, and now it had become a whole different story.

When Richard came back, he shook his head. "No way to trace anything on that. And the number is likely useless, even if we had it. If he's smart, he'll use a different burner phone each time, and then get rid of it."

Just like Gregory had said. Jaxon nodded. "So what am I supposed to do?"

"Watch your back," Richard instructed. "And hers too because this doesn't sound very good at all." He frowned. "From what I just heard, I'm getting that somebody is really pissed off about something."

"Yeah, and, from my point of view, if you guys can't do anything about it—"

"For now we really can't, other than put out feelers for purchases of too many burner phones at once," Richard shared apologetically, "because there's no way to trace that single Private Number call. Even if we could, we would need a whole lot more information. You can hope he stops calling at some point, but, after hearing the message today for myself, I don't see your caller stopping anytime soon."

"It's definitely escalating," Jaxon agreed, trying to keep his frustration down. "So, if you find my dead body on the side of the road somewhere, it's not an accident." And, with that harsh note, he stepped out into the big bad world, wondering who the hell was after him and Keisha and why their harassing caller had gotten so ugly about it. Sure, they were part of a family who died in car accident, along with another family man, but neither Keisha nor Jaxon were at the accident scene. He shook his head.

As soon as he got back to his truck, he contacted Timber and told him what happened.

"That sucks, but they're right. Richard is good at his job, but your caller is pretty savvy, and, until they can grab some concrete evidence, what are they supposed to do?"

"I don't know," Jaxon muttered, "but I don't feel good about leaving Keisha alone, and I certainly don't feel good about some asshole trying to stop whatever it is that we're doing."

"I get that too," Timber noted.

"So, while I'm here in town," Jaxon began, "I'll track down the other family who lost somebody. … They may not want to talk to me though."

"And yet, if they have nothing to do with it, they might not have a problem at all," Timber pointed out.

"At least I have their contact information." With that, he disconnected from Timber, went to a nearby coffee shop, and ordered himself a coffee. Then, from the back corner, he made the call. When a young man answered, Jaxon explained who he was.

"And what do you want now?" Cameron asked, with a yawn and a completely disinterested voice.

"I just wondered how your family was holding up."

"That's a bizarre question, isn't it?" Bitterness filled his tone. "My father was killed in a car accident. What more do you want to know?"

"I understand. My wife's parents were killed in that same accident."

"Yeah, but that damn driver didn't suffer enough," he barked.

At that, Jaxon froze. "What do you mean, the driver didn't suffer?"

"The police all said that a man was driving the other car. However, my father was alive when I initially got to him, and he told me that bitch was driving the other car."

"The mother?"

"No. The one who's paralyzed. So, she gets to live with what she's done, but sometimes it still doesn't seem to be quite enough punishment. My mother would say it's more than enough though," Cameron muttered, with a sigh. "I'm still trying to get over the loss of my dad though, so don't mind me."

"I'm sorry. I realize it was a pretty harsh ending."

"Yeah, you're not kidding," he spat, sorrow in his voice. "My dad was the best, but—"

"Do you think it was deliberate?"

"Oh no, not at all," he replied. "It was an accident. Yet, … as you know, accidents don't make us feel any better. Just because it wasn't deliberate doesn't mean it's easy."

"No, of course not," Jaxon agreed. "I'm sorry. I didn't mean to imply that."

"How is she doing?"

"Not very well," he murmured. "She's struggling in many ways."

"To be honest, a part of me says *good*, and another part of me says that's the wrong thing to say," he admitted. "I know she's in a wheelchair, so that can't be easy on her, but I wonder if she ever even thinks about my dad."

"I can mention it to her, but are you open to having a conversation with her?"

"No," he declared, his tone harsh. "My mother would probably be open to it, but I'm not. I still see him in every room I walk into. I haven't got Mom's fatalistic attitude. She's always saying, *It had to happen sometime.*"

"Did your father have a health condition?"

"Oh, you're not blaming this on him," he stated forcefully.

"No, never," Jaxon confirmed quickly. "That's not why I was asking. Yet what you shared about your mom's attitude sounded like she knew his time was coming, sooner than later."

"He had Type-1 diabetes and was struggling to control it," he explained. "So, if anything, maybe that's what she was talking about. I don't have a clue. I've never thought about it in that way before."

Jaxon didn't say anything to that. Dying from Type-1 diabetes or from a car accident was still fatal either way.

Cameron added, "I've got to go, and I don't know why you even bothered calling. If you want to talk to my mother, I would appreciate you giving me a heads-up first. So I can warn her."

"Of course," Jaxon acknowledged. "I wouldn't want to upset her."

"It's not as if speaking to you about the accident that took her husband will make her feel good though, now will it?" he snapped. "You're dredging up a major loss in her life, losing somebody who she absolutely loved and spent every waking hour with."

"Of course," Jaxon replied.

When Cameron rang off, Jaxon sat here, wondering about what he'd heard. Cameron was a young man, and maybe he had more anger and frustration inside than was obvious, yet nothing in his tone of voice stuck out as threatening. All in all, he sounded more frustrated and missing his dad than anything else.

Their harassing caller *could* have been him, but, as Cameron had pointed out so aptly, Kelly was already in a wheelchair, and that was her punishment. So what would be the point of finally and permanently breaking up Jaxon's marriage to Keisha?

What was most fascinating was the fact that Cameron declared that Kelly was driving. That was something Jaxon needed to follow up on.

He headed to the animal clinic first, wondering just what to tell Keisha, because it wouldn't be an easy conversation. When he walked in, she was just locking up.

"Hey," she greeted him, with a big smile. "I wasn't expecting to see you today."

"No, I just came back from the detective's office."

She stopped and stared at him. "Why? I know you mentioned it before but are you sure it's a good idea?"

"Why what?" he asked. "Why did I go, or why am I back?"

"Either way," she said, frowning at him.

"I wanted to confirm that somebody knew about these phone calls."

She paled as she realized the meaning behind that. "*Great*, not exactly what I wanted to think about today."

"No, I'm sure it isn't," he began, "but certainly you can see why it's something that needed to be brought up. As it is, I got another one of those phone calls while I was still in the police station."

She grimaced. "And could they do anything about it?"

"No." He shook his head. "They did take my phone and

checked it out, but they couldn't get anything, which we pretty much already knew from Gregory."

"Of course," she muttered. "I keep thinking there's got to be something we can do, but I come up with just nothing."

"How about dinner?" he asked. "I'm in town anyway."

"Sure," she agreed, with another smile. "I would love to. There's a new fish-and-chips joint not too far from here, if you're interested."

"Sounds great," he said, with a bright smile. With the clinic all locked up, they used both vehicles to get there, so she could go home afterward, and headed to the new restaurant.

As they walked in, they were given a table right away, even though it was pretty busy. He looked around and noted, "This is a pretty-hopping place, isn't it?"

"I've spoken to several of my staff, and they've all been here and say it's great."

The fact of the matter was, it was midweek, so it was surprising to find it so busy, even for a new establishment. As it was, the employees were moving pretty fast. Keisha and Jaxon had their drinks already, then ordered quickly, as both of them just wanted the main offering, the fish and chips. When the waitress returned in a matter of minutes with their order, Jaxon looked at Keisha in surprise. "Really fast service, wasn't it?"

"That's what they do full-time though," she pointed out. "It's like their main menu, all day, every day, so it makes sense." As they tucked in to eat, she added, "Tell me what the detective had to say."

"So, that would be Detective Richard Martin, and he has military history with Timber and also some police history with some incidents involving the Haven. Richard gave me the details on the accident with your family, and I contacted the other family."

She winced and slowly nodded. "I've often thought about doing that. I've always felt horrible because it wasn't just my sister and my parents who were affected," she acknowledged. "Another family was as well."

He took another bite and nodded.

"How was your reception?" she asked.

"I spoke to the son, Cameron. He mentioned he wasn't nearly as reconciled to it as his mother, who seems to be a lot more fatalistic. In fact, he mentioned her saying something about it being *bound to happen sometime*." Jaxon tilted his head. "But the kid still holds a lot of bitterness. He's clearly still actively grieving the loss of his dad."

She nodded, then asked, "Do you think he's the one sending us harassing phone calls?"

"I didn't get that feeling from him," Jaxon said. "Obviously I don't know for sure, but I didn't get any sense of that level of anger or revenge or retribution or the like. Cameron certainly felt angst over the accident for a whole other reason." He hesitated for a moment, taking a drink of his water. "I don't even know how much to tell you."

"Oh, you need to tell me everything," she declared, throwing her hair off her shoulder. "This is my family."

"I know that, but he shared something that I don't know if you already heard, and it was pretty distressing, even for me."

She immediately sat back and stared at him.

Thankfully she'd already finished her dinner, which was probably a good thing, since she was about to lose her appetite.

"What did he say?" she asked.

"He pointed out that the police report stated that your father was driving."

"Yes," she muttered, sitting up, her back straight, "and he was such a careful driver. I was really surprised they'd been in an accident at all."

Jaxon just nodded.

"Okay, Jaxon. What are you saying or *not saying?*" she asked. "The accident has already happened."

"His father told Cameron something before he passed on."

She frowned. "That's right. I remember he lived for a time but died that night in the hospital."

Jaxon sighed. "The father told Cameron that the young woman was the one driving."

CHAPTER 18

KEISHA STARED AT him in shock. "You're saying that Kelly was driving?"

"No, I'm not saying that. I'm saying that, according to Cameron's father, before he passed away, Kelly was driving."

She stared at him. "Good God."

"According to Richard, it was deemed an accident at the time. And I guess road conditions were not the greatest, or at least there wasn't any reason for anybody to suspect anything else," he clarified. "The accident scene was a mess, as people had been busy trying to get them out of the vehicles because a fire had started. There also wasn't a whole lot of information available, plus the scene had been rearranged, and it was just deemed an accident," he reported.

She stared at him, and he could see that she was trying to process it. Then she started to shake her head, and he could see that some of the truths were starting to land.

"That"—she shook her head again—"that makes no sense."

"Why is that?"

"Because, if Kelly was driving, that means she was at fault."

"Maybe, maybe not," Jaxon clarified. "The weather was bad that particular evening. Maybe it was still just an accident, and maybe it was no one's fault. I don't know how old Kelly was back then, but I remember her as young. Would your parents have let her drive?"

She stared at him, grimacing. "She was trying to get her license. She had her learner's permit at the time but didn't have ..." She shook her head. "Wait, she did have her license." She frowned, as she corrected herself. "She had her license but didn't drive very much."

"And potentially maybe your dad had a drink at a meal wherever they were," he suggested. "I don't even know where they had gone that night."

"I'm not sure I ever knew either. I just know they were all together." She stared at him and muttered, "That really changes things, you know?"

"Does it?" He lifted his head.

The waitress arrived just then with their check. He immediately placed his credit card on the tray, knowing Keisha was already too stunned to even contemplate what he was doing. "I guess one of the questions that needs to be asked is what she meant when she was talking about guilt with you earlier."

"But that would imply she remembers the accident," Keisha noted, staring at him. He just nodded. "She continually tells me that she doesn't remember a thing. Why wouldn't she tell me?" He looked at her, raised one eyebrow, and she winced. "Right, she wouldn't tell me the truth because, in her mind, she would be forever guilty, and there would be no getting over that."

"I don't know about *not getting over it*," he added, "but it would certainly be a much harder prospect."

She sucked in her breath and said, "I need to go home."

He immediately got up and motioned for her to head out to their vehicles, just as the waitress came back with his card. He held up his hand to stop her, quickly signing for the charge to go through, then followed Keisha to the exit.

She just waved her hand. "I'll go home and talk to her." When he hesitated, she looked at him and nodded. "I know. I know. I need to wait until I'm less emotional. I don't want to accuse her of anything, but, if she was driving, the least she could have done was tell me. I get that, in the end, it doesn't matter because of her circumstances, but I also lost my parents that night," she declared.

Jaxon heard the first note of bitterness from Keisha in relation to her sister. He nodded. "And that's one of the reasons I wanted to find out the truth. We also need to find out if this is connected to those threatening phone calls."

She nodded. "Good God," she muttered, hanging her head. "Isn't Kelly in a wheelchair punishment enough? How does this shit happen?"

"Because people don't tell the truth, but then it starts to eat them up from the inside."

She stopped at that, turning to him, her eyes widening. "You're right. That could explain her behavior."

"It might," he conceded, with a nod, "but it's still something that we'll have to deal with."

She gave a broken laugh. "I think everything is something I have to deal with. I just never quite get clear from one problem to the next." He didn't say anything, and, once they were at their vehicles, she looked at him and said, "I can't have you there when I'm talking to her."

"I understand that," he noted, with a smile, "but just prepare yourself, as it'll stir up an awful lot of issues for her."

She winced at that and nodded. "And she could end up back in the hospital. She's not far from ending up in the hospital anyway," she pointed out. "She's definitely not as stable as I would want her to be."

"Maybe this is at least partly why. I doubt if she's ever told anyone."

"No, I doubt if she has either," she whispered.

And, with that, he got into his vehicle and waited until she left, then followed her all the way, knowing it was for his own sake and for her safety. He just couldn't shake the feeling that, somewhere along the line, something had shifted, and there would likely be more of an awakening happening here than any of them anticipated.

When he got to her house, she waved at him as she pulled into her driveway. He waved back, and, seeing that she was safely home, he returned to the Haven.

As soon as he got inside the main cabin, Timber was still up and sitting in front of their scheduling whiteboards.

Timber turned to face him. "And?"

"I don't know." Jaxon shrugged, then explained all that he'd learned, including his visit with Richard, the call with Cameron, and his dinner talk with Keisha. "She'll speak to Kelly about it."

"Is that wise?"

"No, it's probably not wise, but a lot of unfinished business is here. Keisha even pointed out that, in all of this, she's never been able to really deal with the loss of her parents because she's never had a chance to grieve, not with all the Kelly antics," he shared, with a shake of his head. "Everything has always been about Kelly."

"Right," Timber muttered, with a nod. "That makes perfect sense." Then he frowned. "I'm not liking this phone call thing though."

"No, me neither. The fact that it's likely a burner phone, which the police and Gregory both cannot trace, means that

I'm just not getting anywhere."

"Do you think the son had anything to do with it?"

"No, I don't think so," Jaxon stated. "Cameron's still …
I don't want to say angry, but he is bitter. He didn't seem to
hold it against Kelly though, as she's already got enough to
pay for and to live with. So, if she did have anything to do
with the accident, or she had some responsibility involved in
all three deaths, I think Cameron felt she has probably been
punished enough."

"I'm not sure I'm against that either," Timber muttered.
"It's just a shit situation all around."

"It is, and we can't make it any better until we figure out
the truth."

"It'll be pretty ugly for Kelly to confess if she was driving
because, up until now, it's been believed that her father was
at the wheel."

"I know, and, if that's not the case, I don't know if the
police would change their position or not on the accident
report findings."

"Hopefully it would still be deemed an accident, but I
can't be sure," he acknowledged. "The repercussions of
naming Kelly as the driver could be pretty horrific."

Jaxon didn't say anything to that. When his phone rang
shortly thereafter, he looked down and saw it was Keisha.
"Hey, Keisha. Are you okay?"

"Not really," she declared, anger in her voice. "I'm back
at the hospital."

"Oh no, what's going on?"

"She tried to commit suicide," Keisha replied. "I didn't
even get a chance to talk to her. I came inside and thought
she was in bed. I decided to just leave it until tomorrow and
wanted to take the dogs out, but they wouldn't leave her

door. So, I went in to talk to her and found her on the floor. She'd taken a bunch of pills," she spat. "So, here I am, back at the hospital, and this time we need to get to the bottom of it."

"And this time," Jaxon declared, "if she's gone that far, you have grounds to make sure she gets some professional help." He heard Keisha now crying through the phone. "I'll come stay with you."

"No," she immediately replied. "I'll end up here at the hospital the whole night."

"No need to do that since the doctors will have her well in hand. She'll be under constant watch, on *suicide* watch."

"Yes, but I don't feel as if I can leave her."

He didn't say anything and looked over at Timber and shrugged. Timber just nodded. "Okay, but call me if you need anything. Please, just … call me." She thanked him between sobs, and then he disconnected.

Timber muttered, "That didn't sound good at all, and I only heard your side of the conversation."

"Kelly took all the medications she had at home," Jaxon explained. "They've pumped her stomach, and, for now, she's—"

"That was a cry for help," Timber stated immediately. "Now maybe she can get it, in spite of herself."

"I hope so. God, I hope so." Jaxon stared at Timber. "What the hell is going on?"

"I know this is a tough question to ask and is even more insensitive now, but is there any chance that Kelly's the one behind all these phone calls?" Timber asked him.

"I … don't think so," he muttered, frowning at him. "Yet I don't really know that. I don't know that she would even know how to pull it off, with the altered computerized voice and all."

"If she didn't know how, does she have anybody, any friends?"

"I have never seen or heard about a friend," he replied. "So I don't know if she does or not. Particularly after the accident. She's been holed up at home all this time ever since."

Timber pondered that for a long moment. "What about online accounts? That would be important to know about and to look into."

Jaxon winced. "I don't think Keisha would take kindly to that."

"Maybe not," Timber noted, "but, if you asked for permission, you can check if there's something nefarious in her computer or her phone. The fact that she's already done what she's done means that she could have an online group. If she is as isolated as she appears to be, it's quite possible she's got somebody in an online group who isn't doing her any favors."

"Crap," Jaxon muttered, pulling out his phone. He walked several steps away, and, when Keisha answered the phone, he began, "I know this is an imposition and something that will sound absolutely horrible, but—"

"Cut to the chase, Jaxon."

"Okay. Have you considered that Kelly could belong to some group online that's doing her more harm than good?"

"I have considered it," she admitted. "I just don't know how to do anything about it."

"You won't like this, but what if I checked her computer and her phone?" Keisha gasped at that. He continued. "I know. It's a total invasion of privacy, and I wouldn't ask if we didn't have such a major problem."

"I don't even know what to say to that," she cried out.

"She's in the hospital."

"And, for all we know, she could be in the hospital right now because of some online group." Keisha started crying softly. Jaxon shook his head and sighed. "I'm not trying to put you on the spot, but there is a reasonable potential that she's getting some really bad advice online."

"It definitely sounds as if you're trying to put me on the spot," she replied, with some force in her tone, "but I do understand."

He added, "I don't know what to say or how else to get to the bottom of this, but we do have a major problem with Kelly now."

"I get that, but she is just so very unhappy, that's all. And considering her situation, it's understandable. Maybe she just needs some time," Keisha suggested. "Shit, what am I saying? Do you really think that's possible? Jesus, what next?"

"In this case, we have a way to find out one way or another. For sure."

"Some actual facts would be nice," she agreed. "Meet me at the house. You're right. ... We do need to get to the bottom of anything we can, and, if anybody will go through her stuff, it'll be me. She can hate me all she wants, but having done what she's just done, I can't ever leave her alone again, not without checking this out," she stated. "I'll be back there in thirty minutes. Oh, shit. Her counselor was supposed to come see her at home today. I'll call him before I forget all about it."

With that, he disconnected.

Timber nodded. "Not an easy row to hoe," he said, "but you and I have both seen the results of these kinds of injuries."

"I know," he murmured. "And there's been something so off about Kelly's behavior this entire time."

"And her responsibility for the accident could easily be a part of all this. Guilt is like that."

"But then"—Jaxon turned to him—"who the hell is making all these phone calls?"

"Does she have access to your phone number?"

"I'm sure she's had access to it somewhere along the line. She would only have to get a hold of Keisha's phone to see it. And she's bound to have done that."

"So, keep that in mind."

"Right, and that's about the last thing I want to think about."

"I get it, but still … keep that in mind."

On that note Jaxon turned and walked out, heading straight back to town.

CHAPTER 19

KEISHA ARRIVED BACK home, nervous, upset, angry, and determined to get to the bottom of this. She wasn't surprised to find Jaxon sitting outside the house, waiting for her. As soon as she hopped out and walked to the front door, he got up from the steps. "I don't even want to think that something is going on in the background, egging Kelly on," Keisha muttered, walking past him.

"No, but considering her actions tonight, and the fact that this situation is worsening by the day," Jaxon pointed out, "better to find out right now if we should know about anything else."

"She'll be so angry when she finds out about this."

Jaxon shook his head. "And yet everything she's been doing is a cry for help, long before this suicide attempt."

Keisha nodded. "I know that, and I hear you. I get it. One of the nurses mentioned that to me also," she shared, "but it still doesn't make it any easier."

"No, of course not." He walked over to the front door, and she quickly unlocked it, and they both stepped inside. There was an eerie hollowness to it. Only to do a 180 shift as the dogs barreled toward them, barking and jumping with joy.

She crouched down to greet them laughing as they knocked her over in their joy.

When she finally stood, she sighed. "You know, this is *not* where I wanted to stay at all. But, after both my parents were gone, it just seemed to be the easiest solution for Kelly." When he didn't say anything, she looked over at him. "You think it was the wrong decision, don't you?"

He shrugged. "I don't have any thoughts on whether that was the right or the wrong decision. You were doing the best you could in a really tough situation. You just lost your parents, and you were suddenly responsible for your younger sister, who was now in a wheelchair. Keeping afloat with all that going on was huge," he noted, shaking his head, "but you made it work, and that's what counts."

Her shoulders sagged. "I don't know. Considering how it's going, I won't let myself off the hook quite so easily."

"Of course not," he whispered, with a smile in her direction. "You care, and, because you care, it's easy for everybody to twist you around."

"Which shouldn't be a thing," she cried out. "People should be good and decent."

"Sure, but then they get into situations like Kelly's, where they can't see their way out."

"And what has any of this … and Kelly … have to do with these damn phone calls?"

"I don't know," he said, with a smile. "And I don't want to think that she had anything to do with it."

Keisha stared at him. "Oh God, is that why we're here?" she asked in an ominous tone.

He groaned. "We need to figure out what's happening. I don't know what's going on, or who is doing what, but we need to figure it out, and that means we must clear up anything we can."

"Are you seriously thinking she's the one making the calls?"

"I don't know that she is personally. What I'm more worried about is that she might be connected to somebody online who is pushing her to take her own life, potentially someone who has been in the background, pushing her to send these phone calls. I'm not saying she made them, but I'm wondering if maybe somebody around her was making them for her."

Keisha stared at him and shivered. "Are there really people like that out there?"

"Yes," he stated immediately.

She gasped and then closed her mouth and hurried to her sister's room on the first floor. "I don't know why anybody would want to help somebody else take their own life," she muttered.

"Because some people are assholes who get a rush from the power to be had by orchestrating this shit from behind their computers," Jaxon explained. "I have no idea if that's what happened, but we need to figure it out."

He didn't say anything else, as they walked into Kelly's bedroom. Keisha winced because everything was dark. As he turned on the lights, it was obvious that Kelly hadn't been living in a decent mental state for a while.

"Good God," Keisha said, staring around. "I wasn't seeing this before."

"When were you last in here?"

"She doesn't want me in here," she replied, as she bent down to pick up a box of pizza right by the door. "She's been pretty vocal about that too."

"Of course, but that still begs the question, when were you last in here?"

She shrugged. "I brought her laundry in maybe a week or so ago, but I didn't really get a chance to see anything because she got angry that I had entered without her permission. And of course I found her on the floor this morning but again, it's not like I was looking around at anything. I was focused on her."

"How old is she?"

"She's twenty-two, but I don't know that she's way younger in terms of maturity," she clarified, with a note of humor.

"No, of course not, especially if you look at this room right now," he pointed out. "I'm surprised that the wheelchair maneuvers in here as well as it does."

"And I don't know if it does. She can get to the edge of her bed there," she pointed out, "and the rest might just be …" She winced, looking around at the state of everything scattered around the room. "She might just be crawling." When he looked at her, she shrugged. "She's not a big fan of the wheelchair, but she's not a fan of crawling and pulling her legs behind her either."

"That is a very strange scenario," he noted, "but I guess if she prefers it, then it doesn't matter."

"Exactly, and honestly, as long as she was eating and sleeping and functioning on a normal level, maintaining in some way, then I was happy to leave her be. Obviously I'm not thrilled about the state of this room."

The state of the room could mean so much, and in this case none of it was good. It was a complete disaster, and there was literally a pathway to the bed and every other space was covered with dishes and take-out containers.

"I presume she's ordering in," Jaxon suggested, as he pointed around the room.

She frowned and nodded. "Apparently, though I didn't know that."

"So, she's independent financially?"

"She has some money, from the accident."

"Ah." He frowned at that.

"Why the frown?" she asked, watching him.

"Because that money could go toward all kinds of things, including getting her job skills, to keep herself happy and motivated and moving her forward in life," he pointed out, "but I get that it's much easier to just sit back and do nothing."

She groaned. "I'm really not in a position to discuss her mental state."

"Of course not," he agreed, "but it's obvious that she needs some help."

"Yes, but she won't go, so that leaves me with no options."

He didn't say anything more, but he walked over to the computer, tapped the screen, and hit Enter to bring up whatever she had been looking at last. Sure enough, there was an open Chat. He swore as he sat down.

"What's the matter?" Keisha asked.

"Let me see what's here first, and then I'll tell you."

She read over his shoulder and saw somebody was talking to Kelly, as she discussed how much she hated her life and how she didn't want to be here. Keisha winced as she read it. "Good God, she's seriously unhappy."

"Of course she is, and we've seen it in many cases involving veterans," Jaxon shared, "but I was hoping she would pull through."

"There's so much she could do. It's partial, she's a partial paraplegic," Keisha stated, her voice rising as she looked around the room again. "She's got the full use of her hands and her upper chest. She doesn't have full use of her legs, but she can maneuver ever-so-slightly with them."

He didn't say anything, just nodded.

As he scrolled through the Chat, she suddenly realized an odd silence had filled the room. "What's the matter?" she asked.

"This person—in a very subtle way—has been encouraging her to take her life." He pointed out a couple instances. "See here and here? He's telling her, if that's what she wants to do, then maybe her life would be better off that way, and she wouldn't be a burden to anybody."

"Oh my God." Keisha bent down to read it. "That's awful. She isn't a burden."

"No, but she's got in with a group of people here," Jaxon noted, "and I don't want to leave this page because I'm not sure how to get back to it. Nevertheless it looks as if we've got at least one person here who's encouraging her to make choices, pushing decisions that she wants to make, but not necessarily good decisions for her mental health at this point."

He pulled out his phone and started sending screenshots of the conversations to Richard.

When Richard phoned him a little later, he asked, "What the hell is all this?"

"Keisha's sister swallowed a whole pile of pills tonight, so I thought that, while she was away from her computer, we should figure out if anybody online was pushing her into these acts. Those screenshots are part of a Chat conversation I found open on her computer."

"Good God," Richard said. "Not the kind of people you want your sister around, are they?"

"No, and, from the looks of it, she's been sliding down this pathway for quite a few months, if not longer." As he went back as far he could, he added, "It seems things really picked up about the time I came back."

"And that's not your fault," Keisha stated immediately.

"No, not my fault, but certainly could be what sent her down this road."

She groaned. "And that again is not your fault." He didn't say anything, and she heard Richard in the background.

"Give me your address. I'm coming over. I want to take a look at this."

"Good, you do that," he muttered. "I don't know what our legal status is, but, considering that Kelly tried to commit suicide, I'm hoping we get a pass for invading her privacy."

"Yeah, absolutely. Once someone makes an attempt like that, there are all kinds of different legalities," Richard murmured. "Besides, Keisha would be considered her caregiver and responsible adult."

"I'll let you in," Keisha interjected, "just come up to the front door."

He was there within a few minutes. As Richard walked into Kelly's bedroom, he stopped and winced. "Okay, this isn't even a healthy environment."

Keisha sighed. "I know, and you're making me feel even worse about it."

He turned to her and asked, "You work full-time?"

"Yeah, I work full-time. I run my own business, a veterinary practice. I hadn't realized that her mental state was … No." She stopped and looked around the room. "That's not true. I did realize her mental state was an issue, but I didn't realize that she had let her room go like this. I had no idea she was ordering in food, since I cook literally every night.

She's been refusing dinner, but then sometimes the leftovers are gone the next day, and I'm happy because I've been thinking that at least she's eating. Yet apparently *this* is what she's eating." Keisha stared in shock at all the take-out containers.

"And even that is not an issue, providing she has the money to pay her bills, and it's not adding to your credit card debts," Richard suggested, turning to look at her.

She frowned at that. "I'll have to check that out a little further."

He nodded. "Maybe you should do that now." She winced and hunched over a little bit. Richard added, "I'll need some time in here right now."

She nodded and stepped away, realizing that she was essentially being told to leave. When she looked over at Jaxon, he nodded.

"Come on. Let's go make some tea or something."

She let him lead her away, and, as they made it to the kitchen, she asked, "Did somebody really want her to commit suicide?"

"It's not even that they necessarily wanted her to commit suicide, but it's giving them a sense of … power, of being able to manipulate people," he explained. "She's a vulnerable young woman, and, while I don't know all of what's been going on, once you get in with a crowd like that, it's basically bullies and mean girls and cults, which are all hard to be free and clear of to make your own decisions. I know that this isn't the time to bring it up, but look how easily influenced you were by her, once she started browbeating you."

She stared at him, closed her eyes briefly, then nodded. "Yeah. … I really was, wasn't I?"

"And that's not why I brought it up, except to show you

that it can happen and can definitely be an issue."

"Right, … it is. You're right, 100 percent." She stared off in the distance. "How am I supposed to help her?"

"At this point, she needs professional help," he stated, "and I'm not just saying that. You've known it yourself, and she's declined, but now she will be forced to get it."

"I guess." Keisha brushed back her hair. "Do you think Richard wants coffee?"

"I think he would appreciate the gesture, if nothing else. It's late for coffee, but I don't know what his work schedule looks like anyway."

She snorted. "The field that he's in, it probably never ends."

When they brought him a cup of coffee a little bit later, he mumbled something, then paused, looked up, and realized what she'd done. He smiled. "Thank you."

She looked at him and asked, "Did you find anything?"

"I found all kinds of things," he replied, "and none of them good. We've been after a group of people, an online Chat group. They're all over the world, and this isn't the first instance we've heard about. We've certainly been aware that some people are heavily involved in this thing," he shared, taking a sip of his coffee. "So, having access to the Chat right now is a huge boon, and I'm hoping it will give us an opportunity to do something about it." He looked over at her and stated, "I'll need to take her computer in."

She frowned at him.

He nodded. "It's necessary. Plus, we don't want her to come back to this, and we don't want anybody else in this Chat group to do what she did."

She nodded slowly. "Okay. Can she get it back later?"

"Yes, absolutely, but not for a little while. We'll need to

go over everything that we've got here, the whole works."

She sighed. "Okay fine, it's just …"

"No," Richard declared, "it's not an option. This is important."

She nodded. "Fine. … Take it. Just take it. I'll deal with Kelly when I get her home again."

He shook his head. "You need to let the professionals help her from here out."

"I'm not the one stopping them," she said, looking at him in shock. "Detective, I've tried really hard to get her help."

"This attempt will trigger quite a few automatic processes now," he stated, giving her a sideways look, "and you need to let that process happen."

She swallowed hard. "Are you telling me that she's not coming home anytime soon?"

"No, not likely," he said. "At least not for a few days or weeks." She stepped aside as he quickly packed up everything. "I'm taking it all in, and I'll get you a receipt."

She nodded, not sure what the process was, but it was done very quickly. "Where will you take this?"

"To forensics right now." When he loaded everything in his car, he turned back, smiled at her, and added, "We'll get to the bottom of this." And, with that, he was gone.

She looked over at Jaxon. "Not exactly how I thought my night would go."

"Of course not," he muttered, as he put his arms around her, pulling her in for a hug. "Not an easy evening for anybody regardless."

"No, and somehow it just seems worse when I realize I let her get this bad right under my nose."

"Stop that right now," he snapped.

"I know that it's not my fault … and yet—"

"It's simply not your fault," he declared. "It's just not. Kelly is twenty-two."

She smiled. "You're always so supportive."

"I'm supposed to be. In one sense of the word, it's because I am your husband. I'm supposed to be helping you deal with any trauma or trouble. At the same time, I'm also a human being and recognize that you trashing yourself, or blaming yourself for this in any way, won't accomplish anything. You need to understand and to accept that it's not your fault, that Kelly is an adult, even if not as mature as most twenty-two year-olds."

She groaned. "I don't even know how to think about some of this. I still can't really even begin to believe that groups of people are out there encouraging others to hurt themselves. Why would they do that?"

"Possibly because they don't have the self-control, the means, or the willpower to do it themselves," he suggested. "People are using this to empower themselves, which usually means they feel powerless for some reason."

"It's just so terrible."

"It is, and it's also common in a way. People push and try to coerce other people to do all kinds of stuff," he noted. "This is just one of the extreme cases."

"And it's BS," she said immediately.

He smiled. "At least we're in the process of getting Kelly some help, and that is a good thing."

"She won't appreciate it."

"No, but we can't let her make the decisions right now—"

"She brought it on herself. And I do think it's a cry for help, whether she wants to acknowledge it or not. Doing something like this is exactly what that was." Keisha wandered around the house, not even sure what to do or say.

Jaxon asked, "Do you want me to stay here for the night, so you're not alone?"

She hesitated and then looked at him. "Would you mind?"

"Not at all. We did have a relationship, remember?"

"We still do," she said. "I just can't quite define what it is right now."

"Nobody needs to define it," he replied.

She looked over at him. "I was trying to figure it out earlier because, at the bottom of it all, if I truly loved you," she shared, "I would never have done that to you."

He winced. "There is that. Yet you were also dealing with Kelly, who we know now was on a downward spiral, and I wasn't helping."

She snorted. "No, you weren't, but then again, Kelly wasn't helping either. I don't know what I expected," she muttered, with a shrug. "The whole thing is just messed up."

"And again, it's nothing that needs to be resolved today."

She smiled. "Maybe not, maybe not today, but it sure feels as if it's got to be coming soon."

"No, it doesn't," he countered, with a smile. "We don't have to make any major decisions right away about our marriage."

She looked up at him. "You're just afraid I'll make the wrong one."

"You're right. I am," he admitted. "I'm afraid you'll make the decision that terminates what we have. We had to go back to the beginning, not quite the beginning, but we obviously needed to get to know who we are again. Letting go of some of the hurt, letting go of some of the trauma," he stated, with a chuckle, "and figuring out just who and what we are and what we want. That doesn't have to be a quick process."

She smiled. "It would be nice if I had time to sort it out."

"You do have time," he declared. "Nobody is pushing you—but you."

She laughed. "I think that's the story of my life, honestly, but thank you. I don't have much space, but—"

"Is the spare room still here?"

"It is and it isn't," she said, with a cringe. "It's just been for storage."

"Let's go take a look."

And as he walked her upstairs to the spare room, he opened the door, took a look inside, and nodded. "Doesn't look as if anybody's been in here since I was here last."

"It's not like you stayed here long."

"No, but I think I mentioned something about moving in and doing something with the spare room, and it caused Kelly to lose it."

"That's because this was my mother's special room," she noted, with a smile. "It was her sewing room, her craft room. Her space, you know?"

"And I had no way of knowing that, so I didn't realize I would be triggering her."

"I don't know that anybody would have known," Keisha added, "so again, you're not to blame."

"Right." Then he laughed. "Does it seem as if excusing each other from blame is all we're doing lately?"

She smiled. "Sort of. Maybe you are right, and we just need time."

"That's exactly what we need," he declared. He wrapped her up in a hug and gave her a gentle kiss.

Even though she wanted so much more, if she went down that pathway, it would send a signal that would be almost impossible to change at this point. Yet they'd already gotten to that point years ago, so why was she even hesitating? Except that she was still an emotional wreck.

"Go to sleep," he suggested. "Everything will look brighter in the morning."

She looked up at him and winced. "Are you sure? Things are looking pretty-damn gloomy right now." And, with that, she left him in the spare bedroom and walked away. As she got to her room, she looked back at him and added, "I don't even know what I'm doing right now."

He frowned, walked closer, and asked, "What do you mean?"

"I want to be in there with you," she shared, "but I feel as if it would change things completely, and I'm not sure I'm ready for that change."

"Nobody has to make any changes right now," he said, a smile on his face. "And coming in here with me, or me coming in there with you, it doesn't need to be a statement of change. It's just a natural progression of who we are."

She smiled and shook her head. "That sounds like cajoling."

He burst out laughing and grinned. "My door is always open, so, if you want to come in, come on in."

And he stepped into the hallway and walked to his room and left his door open.

CHAPTER 20

JAXON WOKE THE next morning, with a sense of disappointment and yet also with a sense of relief because he was under Keisha's roof, if not in her bed.

If he were honest, it was his bed, but he wouldn't go that far. He'd made progress, and he would maintain that sense of joy and confidence that they had gotten this far. He just needed to help her sort out where she wanted to go, and he hoped she ultimately made a decision that would include him. He could see that they were getting closer, and she was open to the concept, but Kelly was still in the middle of it all.

He got up and went downstairs, made coffee, and, by the time it was dripping, he heard her rummaging around in her bedroom upstairs.

When she came downstairs, she yawned and muttered, "I have to go to work today."

He nodded and smiled at her. "That may be a good thing because at least you'll get a chance to think about something else."

"And yet I feel as if I should go to the hospital."

"If she's awake, absolutely," he agreed, "but you don't have to rush there first thing this morning."

"Are you sure?"

"I've already called," he shared. "She's sleeping peacefully at the moment."

She winced at that. "I guess I can't be upset about that."

"No, you sure can't," he said, with a smile, "and I get that you definitely have some talking to do with her, but maybe you could do it a little later. What does your lunch hour look like?"

She sighed. "Well, … I might be able to shift some things around for that, and I don't really know how busy the afternoon is, but I'll do what I can to get to the hospital." As she walked to the front door, she announced, "I still feel guilty."

"Don't," he replied immediately. "I can go to the hospital, if you want. Obviously we need to take care of the dogs before I go, they have to be upset over the recent changes not to mention the tension between the two of you. Something to consider going forward."

She winced, opening her arms to cuddle Harley who then turned around and sat on her feet. They were quickly joined by Homer. She should just take them to work. Both of them had the personality to deal with people coming and going and honestly their presence might calm the other canine patients coming in. But dealing with her sister was first. She looked up at Jaxon.

"That will likely set her off, and that's not what we need right now."

"No, it isn't, but you could also swing by the hospital on your way to the clinic."

"I was thinking about that," she admitted, "but I'm out of time." She winced as she looked at her watch. "And I know that nobody would object because it's my sister, of course, but I also have appointments to keep and animals that need help too. So let me go to work while she's sleeping.

Then I'll see what I can do about my schedule and go from there." She returned to him, kissed him on the cheek, and asked, "What about you?"

"I'm heading back to Timber's. I'll check in and see what the guys are working on. Hopefully I can help some with the animals out there too."

She nodded. "Tell him I'll come out this weekend sometime."

"Nope. I'm not telling him that," he declared, with a raised eyebrow. "He knows perfectly well what's going on and that you'll get there when you can get there. I'm sure Tiffany can cover anything urgent."

"Now, if all my patients were so easily directed," she quipped, "I wouldn't have any problems."

"So, let's hope you have a good day."

As soon as he watched her walk out, both dogs with her for their first day at the office trial, he went back to Kelly's room and took another look around. He wasn't sure exactly what was in the back of his mind, but he definitely had that feeling that, if she had been hiding as much as they'd discovered so far, what else could she have been hiding?

When he found copies of credit card receipts, they weren't Kelly's at all. The cards were in Keisha's name, and he realized that Kelly had been using Keisha's money and not her own for all these take-out meals.

He frowned and shook his head, knowing Keisha would need to take a look at her accounts and assess the damage. Hopefully it was only the takeout, but he wouldn't put anything past Kelly at this point.

Kelly had her own money apparently. Keisha had indicated she was getting some money, but he didn't know if it was an insurance settlement or some disability payments, but he didn't know just how far that would go when it came down to a new life and future job training for Kelly. Taking photocopies of some of the credit card receipts, he headed down to the animal clinic. When he walked in, the dogs greeted him like they hadn't seen him in days. Keisha walked out of her office and toward the reception, saw him and frowned.

"She's fine," he said. "I just needed to talk to you for a moment."

She led the way to her office but said, "Sorry, but I'm really busy, so I don't have long."

"That's fine, but take a seat. You need to look at these." He held out the statements. "You'll need to check your accounts because it looks as if Kelly's been using your credit cards."

"What?" She stared at him in shock, snatched the copies from his hands, and then sagged down into her chair. "Good God. Why would she do this? She has her own money."

"I'm not sure, but I suspect that the same people she's been online with have probably encouraged it, you know, so they can help her *stick it to you because you're the one who's alive and healthy.* My real concern is that she might have been paying somebody or giving away money to people like this."

She stared at the statements. "Jaxon, I don't recognize this. It's not my credit card."

"But your name is on it."

She let out her breath with a hard sigh. "I don't even know what to do with this."

"You need to contact Richard."

She handed them back to him. "Would you take those to him, please? I can't have this happening. My whole clinic could be affected by this.”

“I know, which is why I’m here.”

“Please, just …” She rubbed at her face, clearly overwhelmed.

He nodded. “I’ll go talk to the detective and take these to him. You work on your day and get these animals taken care of.”

She closed her eyes for a brief moment, then slowly opened them. “The animals have always been my salvation,” she noted, “and today won’t be any different.” And, with that said, she stood up, squared her shoulders, then walked out and headed to see the next patient.

As he walked past the front counter, the receptionist asked him, “Is she all right?”

He shook his head. “Not really. It’ll be a rough couple days.”

Tania winced. “She needs a break. It’s been a *rough couple days* for a very long time now.”

“I don’t know if you know what happened with her sister yesterday—”

“I heard.”

“I guess everyone heard, but now there’s a little more to it, which I’m not free to share with you,” he admitted, “but it’ll just add to Keisha’s and Kelly’s problems.”

She winced, then nodded. “That’s the last thing Keisha needs.”

“Keep an eye on her.”

With that, he headed out, went straight to the police station, and, as soon as he had a chance to talk to Richard, he handed over both the original receipts and the copies of the credit card receipts. “I went back to the sister’s bedroom this morning and took another look. These credit card receipts are in Keisha's name, but these aren't credit cards that she knows about."

Richard stared at them and shook his head. "That's a whole different story."

"I know, but what I don't know is whether any of these online friends of hers are getting her to do this or if there are other charges we don't yet know about. Depending on how extensive this credit card theft is, this could really hurt Keisha, even her clinic."

"Does Keisha know?"

"Yeah, I showed these to her at her clinic before coming here. She's the one who asked me to bring you these documents."

Richard flipped through the originals, matching them to the copies. "Somebody needs to call the credit card companies and shut these down."

"And I can't do that because, of course, they're not in my name," Jaxon replied.

Richard nodded. "I can do it because they're part of a fraud investigation. At least they are now," he declared, his tone turning serious. "Jesus, does Kelly not understand how this could impact Keisha's future?"

"I don't think she's given any thought to anyone but herself."

"I agree with that," he stated, "but it's always hard on the family when they find out just how far down the situation has gone."

"And who knows? That could be why she did what she did last night."

"Yeah." Richard scratched his chin. "Okay, leave it with me, and I'll touch base with her this afternoon."

"Good enough," Jaxon replied. "Is there some way for

you to access Keisha's financial records, to see if other debt is being run up in Keisha's name?"

"Maybe, I'll find out."

And, with that, Jaxon had to be satisfied. He turned and walked out, knowing that, for Keisha, it was a whole new day, and none of it would be good.

CHAPTER 21

KEISHA JUST STARED at Jaxon and shook her head. "I can't believe it. … I can't. Kelly wouldn't do that."

He didn't say anything, just waited.

Keisha repeated it, staring at him. "She would never do that. She knows how hard I work."

He shrugged. What could he say? The evidence was here, the proof was here, but she didn't want to believe it. He could well and truly understand, but it didn't change the facts.

She sagged onto her living room chair both dogs backed up and half on her, as if protecting her from the blows they didn't understand. Her emotions, shock… those they understood. "She really racked up all those credit cards?" she whispered.

He nodded. "Yes, and we're still searching to see if there's anything else she put in your name."

She winced at that. "And the whole time, she's staying here, doing nothing to help, just—"

"Yep," he agreed immediately, wanting to cut off the tirade, listing all the things Kelly had done and not done.

"I need to talk to her," Keisha declared, bounding to her feet.

"I understand why you would want to, but it's not a good idea. The detective clearly stated that you let him speak to Kelly first," he repeated.

She stared at him. "That's not good. That'll just send her into another spiral."

"Maybe, but at least she's in the hospital, under constant watch. Plus, we can't make any real progress if we don't know what the whole truth is."

She winced at that. "And you assume there's more?"

"I don't know," he admitted. "Until we get all the information, there isn't a whole lot we can do except worry and wonder, and that's not good for anyone."

"I still have to ask her about all these things myself."

"Yes, and, as long as Richard speaks to her first and she's willing to talk to you, you can."

"Why wouldn't she talk to me?" she cried out in shock.

"Think about it."

She sagged back, and tears filled her eyes. "God, I just don't understand what sent her down this spiral."

"Yes, … you do," Jaxon countered. "What we don't yet understand is how far down she went and what the repercussions are from all that she's done."

"It's just so stupid. Did she really think that I wouldn't eventually find out about the credit cards?"

"I don't know," he replied, "but it could be she thought that day was coming soon, so she would just spend whatever she wanted and then … *check out.*"

At his phrasing, she gasped, and the tears once again filled her eyes. "I don't care about the credit cards," she cried out.

"I know that," he replied, "but the credit cards might just be the tip of the iceberg, and, if we don't have all the information, she can't heal, because nobody will be calling her out on it. We both know she needs more help than she's been getting."

"She's refused to go," Keisha wailed. "I've tried everything."

"I know, but this suicide attempt was likely a cry for help, and now she'll get it, whether she agrees to it or not."

Keisha took several deep breaths. When her phone rang, she looked at the Caller ID and said, "It's the detective." She answered with a wobble in her voice.

He began, "Hello, I'm with your sister. You'll need to come down and join us."

"Great," she said, even with some enthusiasm. Kelly wanted to talk to her, so that was good, right?

"No, not great, not great at all," he stated, with caution in his tone. "However, it needs to happen."

Keisha sat up straight, noting the officious tone to his voice. She winced and asked, "Can Jaxon come?"

"Yes, absolutely." Then he ended the call.

She got up slowly, looked at the time, and told Jaxon, "I just got off work. This is my evening off."

"Doesn't matter, since it is what it is. What's going on?"

"Richard wants me to come down to the hospital, right now."

Jaxon walked over, gave her a hug, and said, "Let's go."

"Maybe we shouldn't have looked at her computer."

Jaxon asked, "Do you want her to heal?"

"Yes," she cried out immediately, then she sighed.

Since Jaxon was driving, she could allow herself to just sag into the passenger seat and think about everything that had gone wrong in the last few years. "It was so hard after the accident."

"Of course it was," he agreed, "for both of you, but she's only focusing on herself and taking it out on you."

"Yeah, but she needs to focus on herself. It's the only

way she'll heal."

"True, but focusing on herself doesn't mean hurting those around her."

Keisha gave him a sad smile. "I think that's exactly what it means, at least in so many cases. If all they can think about is the fact that their life has been damaged, they keep score and compare, taking the role of victim, which starts a circle of hate."

"It doesn't have to be that way. It should be a circle of gratitude that somebody is there to help them."

"Sure, in a perfect world. I haven't seen a perfect world yet, have you?" The bright smile he sent in her direction made her nod. "That's the problem, right? We all know what we want to see happen, but that doesn't mean that we do it."

"No, not as often as we would like to see it," he confirmed.

When he pulled up in front of the hospital, she got out and looked over at him. "Are you sure you want to come?"

"I think I need to come," he noted, with a smile for her. "Considering the state you're in, it's probably better if I'm there."

"She won't like it."

"Depending on what Richard has already told her, she probably won't like anything."

"Yeah, you're right about that," Keisha muttered. "I'm a little worried about what he has to say." Holding hands, they walked into the hospital, found out where Kelly was, and headed up to her room.

"You didn't come by or talk to Kelly earlier?"

"No, she was sleeping when I called, and they told me to check in later."

"And did you check in later?"

"Yes, but I was told she had not fully recovered."

"In other words, she's avoiding you."

"Crap," she muttered. "I was really hoping not to consider that."

"You might be trying to avoid it, but, as you can see, you're about out of time."

When they got to Kelly's room, they knocked and pushed open the door. Detective Richard stood up from where he'd been sitting, smiled at them, and waved them in. "Hey, thanks for coming."

The smile might have been friendly, but his tone was definitely not. Keisha hunched her shoulders and walked up to her sister in the hospital bed, but Kelly kept her head facing the window and wouldn't look at her. "Kelly," Keisha asked, "what's going on?" Kelly didn't say anything, and Keisha looked over at Richard. "Can you explain?"

"You mean, outside of the fraud that your sister has committed? Let's review what we know so far. She has the one card that we confiscated, and two other cards that she just applied for. Then there is the money that she has been giving to a group that apparently needed it for something— except she used your money for it."

She winced at that. "That's *great*," she muttered, with a dry laugh. "I barely have enough money to keep us going as it is, so I don't know what I'm supposed to do about that."

"The credit card companies have been informed about the fraud, so we'll see what they say," Richard noted. "The bottom line right now is that Kelly has committed fraud. She's in trouble for that, and she's also not cooperating when asked for information about a group she belongs to online. If she refuses to talk, we will have to arrest her."

"Because they're not criminals," Kelly snapped. "You're

making it sound as if they're terrible."

Keisha walked over to the other side of Kelly's bed, where her sister stared out the window, and asked, "Are these the people who convinced you to do all this?"

Kelly flushed.

"Are these the people who told you it was okay to open credit cards in my name and to rip me off, even though you know very well that I already work incredibly long days, and that it's all I can do to put food on the table, to pay the mortgage, and to keep you as safe as you need to be?" Keisha asked, her voice breaking.

Kelly flushed again and for the first time looked as if maybe she had some acknowledgment of having done something wrong, but she sure wasn't remorseful. "Maybe," she muttered, "but that still doesn't mean they're bad people."

"*Right.*" Keisha laughed. "So, they are happily working members of society, doing everything they can to be better people, right?"

"Nobody is trying to be better people," Kelly snapped in a scathing retort. "Everybody is out there just to rip each other off."

"Oh, like you ripped me off, you mean?" Keisha asked, looking at Kelly.

Her sister stared out the window, refusing to have anything more to do with the conversation. Keisha turned and looked at Richard.

He smiled at her and continued. "There are obviously a lot of extenuating circumstances here, but there's also a much deeper issue."

"What do you mean?" Keisha asked.

"The group that she belongs to is a group that law enforcement has had our eyes on for a while," he admitted. "We've known that somebody out there was encouraging people to do things like this, to harm themselves, but we haven't ever been able to catch them. And now we've got a line on them. So the task force assigned to work on that issue has control of the matter."

She nodded slowly. "And what happens to Kelly?"

"I don't know what local charges will be filed. I'll have to talk to the DA about that."

"And it's all related to the credit card fraud?" Keisha asked.

He nodded.

"So, if I say I don't want to press charges?"

He looked at her intently and then at Jaxon, his eyes squinting. "In that case, *you* will be liable for *all* the charges," he stated. "So, before you decide that you really want to let this go, you may want to take a look at how much the total is."

"How much is it?" she asked warily.

When he told her the five-digit number, she sagged onto the chair beside her sister's hospital bed and whispered, "Good God, Kel."

He nodded. "And keep in mind, this is only what we've found so far."

"What can you do about the charges?" Jaxon asked, putting a hand on Keisha's shoulder. Kelly stared at them, fire in her gaze.

"So, we've alerted the credit card companies to the fraud we've found, but now that we have the fraudster," he shared, "it's doubtful that anybody will let you both off the hook."

Keisha closed her eyes and slowly rubbed her face as he continued.

"Beyond that, I don't know what else Kelly may have done, but there's another twist with the money that she's been handing over to this group. It seems they're also supporting various other groups."

"And is she in trouble for supporting them?" Keisha asked warily.

"We're still investigating to determine the extent of her involvement," Richard replied. "So, whether she's an innocent victim or an active participant has yet to be determined."

Keisha felt the tears in her eyes as she gazed at her sister. "How could you ruin your life like that, Kelly?"

In a move so fast that everybody reared back, Kelly pivoted up onto her elbows and glared at her. "Ruin my life? That happened a long time ago. God, don't you get it? I'm the one who's stuck in the wheelchair. I'm the one who has no life. And what did you do? You went and brought that ass of a husband right back into your world," she snapped, followed by a snort. "I don't even get options like that. I'm a cripple, remember?"

Keisha stared at her sister, clearly seeing the hate for the first time. Not just depression but absolute hate. "It was an accident," she replied, "the kind of thing that can happen to anybody at any time."

Her sister started to shake violently, her anger growing.

"But it wasn't just an accident. You were driving," Jaxon interjected. "So, maybe that accident is something that you feel guilty over."

Her sister's gaze widened. "Where did you hear that?" she whispered.

"From the other family who lost a father," Jaxon stated.

"Is it true?" Keisha asked, shock on her face. Kelly paled

and sank back, but Keisha went on. "Apparently the police didn't put that in the accident report, or maybe they thought you had suffered enough. I don't know. However, I do know that we can't work on your healing until we know the truth. All of it."

"You don't want to know the truth," Kelly snapped.

"So, is the truth that you caused the accident and killed Mom and Dad?" The shock was numbing Keisha, but she also knew just how horrifyingly painful this conversation had to be for her sister because it was absolutely killing Keisha.

Jaxon's hand gently patted her shoulder and slowly rubbed her back.

She took several deep breaths as Kelly stared at her. As the moments ticked by in silence, her sister's mouth opened and closed, as if to say something. She gasped back and forth several times before finally sagging into the hospital bed, as her tears flowed uncontrollably.

"Say it," Keisha stated, refusing to let her sister off the hook on this one. "At least acknowledge the truth of what really happened."

"Fine. I was driving," she roared, bawling her eyes out, "and Dad was making me so angry because he told me that I was speeding. He wanted me to slow down because the road conditions were shit. But instead … because I was so angry at him, I sped up. I lost control. The road conditions … It was horrific," she whispered, with a gasp. "I was too arrogant, too full of myself, and far too angry. We'd had a conversation during dinner that upset them, and I just took that anger out onto the road," she admitted, through her tears. "So, yeah, I killed them, and, yeah, I deserve absolutely everything I get." And, with that, she sobbed even more.

At that point, one of the nurses came inside, took a look around, then suggested that everybody leave the room.

CHAPTER 22

J AXON HELD KEISHA in his arms, the antiseptic smell of the hospital permeating everything around them. He didn't say anything. He just held her. He felt her trembling all the way down her body, as the realization hit and slowly sank in. She hadn't yet started to cry, but he knew that would be the next thing, if she could let herself. What was happening right now was painful to see and made everything else so much worse.

He looked over at Richard, who nodded at the two of them. "I gather at least some of that was news to you."

Keisha just nodded but didn't lift her head off Jaxon's shoulder. Then she spun and looked at Richard and asked, "Did you know?"

He shook his head. "No, I didn't. … I'll stay in touch." Richard turned and walked away, leaving them in Kelly's hospital room, with the nurse attending Kelly.

Jaxon continued to just hold Keisha until the tears came. And finally, when she had her fill, she tilted her head back. "Let's go home."

He nodded, then led the way back out to his vehicle, and, within a few minutes, he was parking outside her house. She looked at him and asked, "Could you please come in?"

He immediately turned off the engine, walked her up to the front door, and led her inside. "Want some tea?" he asked, sitting her down.

"I don't think tea will fix what's wrong in my world," she noted.

"No, it won't, but it might bring a few moments of comfort," he suggested, patting her cheeks. "Your world has been flipped upside down, but it's merely adjusting to a change of news. It's not starting the process all over."

"Rehashing the accident, finding out the truth of it all? It feels raw, as if the healing I had done is gone, and it's all been exposed again."

He didn't say anything, just nodded, and added, "I'll make a cup of tea."

She nodded. "Make me one too, and I'll give it a try."

He made them each some tea, and, when he brought it out, she was sitting on the deck outside, the dogs at her feet. He put her cup of tea beside her, pulled the other chair a bit closer, and sat down next to her.

As they sat quietly, she finally spoke. "I didn't even ask. I was so concerned about her and so traumatized by everything that went on, it didn't even occur to me to ask. And I didn't want a copy of the police report. I didn't want anything." She looked over at him and asked, "Do you think I knew? Even if just subconsciously?"

He looked at her and shrugged. "Maybe you did. Maybe you didn't. It doesn't matter. Either way, Kelly didn't come clean about what happened, and it was ruled an accident, so you all moved forward in a really difficult situation the best you could. Now some years have passed, and obviously something was interfering with her healing, and now we know what it was."

"The guilt," Keisha declared, with a headshake. "It was crippling her far more than her physical injuries."

"Yes, it was, and now maybe, with some long-term professional help, she'll move forward and deal with this." Jaxon hesitated before adding, "You do know that she will most likely end up in a psychiatric hospital in lieu of a prison, right? And, with the growing amount of her fraud, she may be there for years. Although she'd have to be assessed for that. Still prison is on the table too and that could be much harder on her."

Keisha sighed heavily again. She reached out a hand, and he immediately linked his hands with hers. "I'm so sorry for everything I put you through," she muttered. "That was so not fair to you."

"No, but I think we're in a better place for it."

She smiled. "You always were way too understanding."

"I was, except for when I came home and realized how much everything had changed, including you," he shared. "That was a shock for me."

"And not a good one, I'm sure."

"I was still glad to be home, but it was certainly a huge wake-up call to realize that you had changed, that I had changed, and that Kelly? ... Well, that was definitely a change, and nobody was really capable of moving forward at that point." He took a deep breath, looking out into the darkness. "We're all in a very different space right now, and hopefully good things will happen now."

She smiled at him. "I don't even know when I decided that a divorce was a good idea," she admitted. "I think I was just so overwhelmed that I couldn't see a way forward. I needed to clear away things that were causing me stress and pain, and according to my sister ..." She gave a broken laugh.

"Yep, per Kelly, that was all on me." He smiled. "And

you can see why she didn't dare have anything in her world change, fearing that all this would come out or that she would be put out on her own because, in her mind, she felt she deserved it."

Keisha groaned. "I know that all of this will make sense somewhere along the line, and, over time, things will improve, and it won't be quite so painful," she admitted. "But right now? … Wow."

"Do you blame her for your parents' deaths?"

She hesitated at that and then sighed. "No, I don't really blame her for that. While she made a terribly foolish mistake, it was an accident. And I guess since they've been gone for a few years now, everything just feels very disconnected."

"And maybe that's a good thing," Jaxon noted. "You can look at it a little more dispassionately because it did happen a few years ago. It's still like having the scar ripped open, yet you can also see how much damage it's done to her."

Keisha swallowed at that comment. "You're right. … That's a good way to look at it. I could see everything she was going through, but I didn't know how to get through to her."

"You also knew that she needed help, but she wasn't willing to participate."

"Exactly. I could take her to see a therapist or a shrink or even to the grocery store or to the clinic, but she would clam up or act out or flat-out be rude to everybody. I couldn't do anything about it. That was a hard thing because the help was there, but she was unwilling to take advantage of it."

"Because she didn't think she deserved it."

"That and she was terrified the truth would come out." Keisha took a deep breath, picked up the cup of tea, and had a sip, then smiled. "This was a good idea, and it is a comfort. It was something that my mother used to do when there were times of trouble too," she added, with a smile.

"How do you think your parents would want you to handle this?"

"They would tell me to help her, to let all the bad feelings go, and just help her because she's the one who really needs it."

"Did you ever feel as if you didn't count and that she was more important?"

"No, … gosh no," she said. "We were all very close, but she was much younger than me and in a more rebellious stage. I have no idea what the fight at the restaurant would have been about."

"She probably doesn't remember either."

Keisha gave a broken laugh. "That is probably quite true. She always had this capacity to forget everything and to get over being angry very quickly. It took me much longer to get over things," she admitted, with a headshake. "It just makes you wonder how any of this could have happened, you know?" He sat and just let her ruminate. Then finally she added, "I don't know what will happen with her."

"I don't know either, but, because of the attempt on her life, I would presume they'll take her someplace to evaluate her mental state and to give her the assistance that she needs," he suggested.

"And my credit cards," Keisha wailed, suddenly putting down the cup. "God, … I can't pay that all off."

"We don't know what will happen with that. I think, as Richard noted, it'll depend on the credit card companies."

"It's a terrible thing to have to deal with," she murmured.

"And maybe that was all about punishing you too," he said, "because Kelly really was unable to come to terms with the fact that her world had changed to the extent that it had, so she lashed out, punishing you for not even being in the situation."

"And yet, if I had been here and if I had been the one driving, it could just as easily have been me who was paralyzed—or dead."

"Would you have sped up if your father had told you to slow down?"

She looked at him, then immediately shook her head. "No. I would never have gone against my father like that. He was a good man, and, if he told me to do something, I did it. And it wasn't hard because it was always the right thing to do."

"In this instance Kelly didn't do the right thing, and she lost control of the vehicle. That is something she'll be dealing with for the rest of her life. So the real question is, can you forgive her?"

"Yes, absolutely," she stated, looking at him. "I won't have a problem forgiving her for that. I think she'll have a problem forgiving herself."

"I think she already is," he pointed out immediately.

As they sat here for a long moment, she added, "I guess, if the credit card companies can see their way to count this as fraud and to not hold me accountable, I wouldn't press charges."

He was silent for a long moment. He wasn't surprised by her decision, and he wasn't even sure how he felt about it. Had Kelly suffered enough for what she'd done? He didn't know, yet it wasn't in him to judge her when he and many of his friends had very difficult times coming to terms with changes in their worlds too.

She looked over at him. "I guess that makes you disappointed in me, doesn't it?"

Surprised, he shook his head. "That isn't even on the table," he declared.

Keisha nodded. "I guess the question is, will she learn something from it, or will she just fall back into the same pattern down the road?"

"I tend to doubt that she will because there'll be help for her now," he noted, "and she doesn't have to protect her secret anymore. I would like to think that, at some point in time, she would make some restitution to you over all this, but, if not, and you can let it go, then more power to you," he shared.

"And you won't hold it against her?" He frowned at that. She nodded. "See? It's not quite so easy, is it?"

"She's not my sister," he stated, "but she hurt somebody I love."

"Ouch," she muttered.

"She's your sister, so, for me, the forgiveness comes from a very different space. Can I find it? Yes. Will it be today?" He watched her closely. "No, but can I get there? I can," he replied. "Life is too short for that kind of problem. She caused me a lot of grief and nearly caused me to lose the one thing in my life that I absolutely adore. However, she's also the reason that we are much closer again."

She stared at him, then started to laugh. "That sounds very much like a *you* comment."

"It is a *me* comment," he agreed, with a grin, "because that's exactly what's happened."

"It is," she confirmed. "Although she isn't responsible for us getting back together. Yet I do understand how it might feel that way to you." He just smiled and didn't say anything. She sighed heavily. "I just want everything back the way it was."

Then she stopped. "I guess that means wanting my parents back, wanting the accident not to have happened, wanting my sister healthy and on her feet, and none of that will happen," she noted, with a shrug. "I know that. It's just that, if there were such a thing as wishes, and I could make that come true, that would be what I would want."

"And I would want that for you too," he said. "So, where are we at, as a couple?"

"I want to think that we're together," she replied.

"And the divorce papers?"

She laughed. "They've been sitting on my desk because I haven't signed them."

He stared at her. "Wait. I thought *I* was the one who hadn't signed them."

"Maybe it's a case of both of us had things that needed to change, and both of us were looking for reasons to not have to sign," she shared, with a smile. "I realize now that divorce was never what I ever really wanted. I just needed space. I needed a chance to figure out what the hell was spiraling out of control in my world and how to stop it."

"And I don't object to that," he noted, with a laugh. "As long as it means there is room for me in your life."

"Of course there is," she confirmed, with a smile. "You were never intended to be out of my life."

"Good, then no more talk about divorce," he declared immediately, "and no talk about where we are. We're married. That's where we are. You probably need to accept that your sister may still have some issues with that."

"Yeah, she probably will," she said, "but that'll be her

issue, not mine."

"I'm glad to hear that," he noted, with a smile.

She looked over at him, squeezed his fingers, and said, "I really am sorry."

"Hush," he whispered. "We are where we are meant to be, and, other issues aside, that's a good place to be."

CHAPTER 23

A N HOUR OR more later she squeezed his hand and said, "Come on. It's bedtime. I don't know about you, but I'm exhausted."

"Of course you are," he agreed, as he stood up, collected their teacups, and walked into the kitchen.

She locked up the front and back doors and headed upstairs to her bedroom, Jaxon following her. She asked, "Do you think Richard will find whoever did all the calling on our phones?"

Jaxon nodded. "I'm hoping so. I suspect it's someone from the same group, since we found texts and messages where she gave them my number."

She stiffened at that. "I didn't even get to the point of asking her if she was getting those calls too. It's just awful to find out that she was the one behind it."

"She had one degree of separation, since she wasn't doing it herself. She had other people doing it for her."

"But that also means she knew it was happening."

"Yes, and what we don't know is to what extent any of this has gotten to."

"Meaning?"

"I just don't know if more has been planned, outside of just phoning us."

"Why would you even think that?"

"We were threatened, remember?"

"I'm not likely to forget," she said, with a shudder. "Do you think Kelly knew about that?"

"I don't know. I just don't have an answer for that."

"And it didn't come up today at all?"

"No, and that's because Richard is still working on that one," Jaxon pointed out. "Once threats are made, things start to escalate quickly."

She groaned. "I just want it to all go away." As she walked to her bedroom, he stopped at the spare room, one eyebrow raised. She smiled at him. "Like you said, we're married."

"I don't want to push anything."

"I know that, and I'm far too tired for any hanky-panky tonight, but I am absolutely looking forward to sleeping in your arms." His delighted smile made her heart ache for all the pain she had caused. The tears came readily to her eyes.

He immediately shook his head, as if understanding exactly what she was feeling. "No, don't even go there. It's fine."

She sniffled slightly and walked into the bedroom, then quickly shed her clothing, tossing them into the laundry hamper, grabbed a soft nightie, and headed to the bed.

He'd already flipped back the covers the way he always did, and she smiled. "There are just some things you get used to when you sleep with somebody," she noted, "and I have to admit, when I didn't have you around, and I had to do that myself, it just didn't have the same feel."

"Of course not." He smiled in her direction. "It's something you do to show someone you love them."

She felt the tears building up once again. Refusing to let them get away from her, she immediately wiped them away, then crawled into bed, pulled up the covers, and waited for him to join her.

He was a little bit longer in the bathroom, and, when he came back out again, she sighed as she saw his leg.

He nodded. "You never did tell me if it bothered you."

"Of course it doesn't bother me," she said, with a shrug. "It didn't even occur to me that maybe I could have helped you."

"Don't need help," he stated, "and, if I do, I'll let you know."

"Would you though?"

"Absolutely," he declared, facing her. "Because learning to ask for help is a whole different ball game now, and it's something I do need every once in a while. I couldn't even get the damn prosthetic off the other day. I would have loved to have you around to give me a hand."

She giggled at that. "I can just imagine what that looked like."

"It wasn't fun from my side," he admitted, as he slid under the covers and pulled her up against him, tucking his chin at the top of her head. "Now get some rest. You really need it after today's events."

"It is what I need," she agreed, "but I'm still struggling with the whole concept of Kelly's involvement in all that fraud."

"I understand, and again it goes back to her mental state. Trying to hold in the secret of the accident was getting harder, as if it was getting bigger by the day. You can imagine that she was afraid that you would blame her, afraid that you would hate her."

"So, what then? She sets these people up to threaten me?"

"Yep." He tightened his arms around her and whispered, "We'll work it out tomorrow."

She took several long slow breaths, trying to relax, and muttered, "At least I don't have clinic hours tomorrow."

"Good, so maybe we can go back out to the ranch and take a look at those llamas."

"Oh, I do have special feed for them that I want Timber to try."

"Good, another reason to go."

She smiled. "I talked to one of the suppliers too and told him all about the place, and he seemed quite interested in helping out with feed."

"That's even better," he added, with a smile. "We need as much help as we can get."

"We?" she repeated in a teasing voice.

"Yeah, we," he confirmed.

She felt the smile of his lips up against her hair. "You really like that place, don't you?"

"I like the concept, and I like what Timber is doing. I appreciate what he's doing, both for the animals and for the people," he explained, rubbing her back. "So, yeah, I kind of love it."

"Do you see yourself doing something there long-term?"

"I don't know. I'm not exactly sure what I could even do there. Timber can't afford to hire us full-time, and I wouldn't want to put that onus on him anyway."

"And yet you know he'll need people full-time soon."

"It's not something that we've talked openly about, but it is something he has alluded to. I think he's still trying to figure out what happened, when so many people showed up and all the buildings went up so quickly. He's been really struggling to stay on top of his finances and to figure out where he's at."

"Except for Burke's partner, Shirley, she's helping with that, right?"

"Yes, that's a whole different story," he said, laughing. "She worked as a project manager before. So, when she needed a safe place to stay and ended up at the Haven, she naturally fell into that role. She was legitimately just helping him get organized, but she's kind of taken over his life."

"It seems she's really helping him get organized."

"More so than he ever thought possible. Things are running more smoothly, in terms of materials being available when needed, not having to do a job twice because of a missed detail, better allocation of the guys' skills, and that sort of thing. Timber's got some meetings coming up with his financial advisors on investments and stuff."

"Does he have a lot of money?" she asked curiously. "Even with all the volunteer labor you all have been providing, it's still got to be an incredible expense to set up everything needed for big and small animals, especially with all the new land he just acquired."

"I think he has a lot of debt," Jaxon clarified. "I don't think he thought it would go crazily out of control like it has. His original plan was to do all the building himself, alone, but, when free help just shows up, you automatically turn around and find things for everybody to do. I also know that some of his friends who came out initially covered some of the early supply bills. For example, they covered all the food when he had that huge crew out there that first week or two. That was a huge gift."

"He has great friends," she noted, with a smile.

"Indeed, and you might want to remember that they're Tiffany's friends now too."

"Meaning?" she asked, as she yawned.

"That they're your friends now too." He nuzzled her neck under one ear.

She felt his warm breath on her skin and lay there with a smile on her face, contemplating just how wonderful it was to be back in his arms, and, with that, all thoughts of sleeping fled. She rolled over slowly, looked up at him, and smiled. "I'm not feeling quite so tired anymore."

He nuzzled her and shifted down, dropping kisses along her temple, across her cheek, and to her lips. That first kiss reminded her of that same first kiss they had shared so long ago.

With tears in her eyes, she reached up for more, as he tried to withdraw. She whispered, "Please don't stop. I'm so sorry, just so sorry."

He immediately shook his head, cutting off her words with a kiss, letting her know that they weren't required. Yet, in her heart, she knew she would be spending a long time trying to earn his forgiveness, knowing that she was the one who had broken them up and who had caused so much pain for Jaxon. Even though her reasons were for her own sanity, it wasn't something that she'd really wanted to do, and she regretted it terribly.

She wrapped her arms around him and held him close, as their lips made a bond, a seal she had thought she would never experience again. The tears flowed freely, even as he tried to kiss them away, and she just sobbed and sobbed, yet she was smiling with joy.

She finally rolled over, pushing him flat on his back, then spent the next little while slowly memorizing his body, a body she thought for sure she could never forget. Yet every new discovery gave her great joy, coming at her from all directions, as she realized just how much she had missed this, had missed him, and had missed how good everything had always been between them.

She didn't know when she'd forgotten it all or when it had all slipped away. She just remembered the myriad pain and anguish. But it didn't matter now because he was here, because he was with her, and because they had worked their way through the difficult times. She could only hope for good times ahead, but she took comfort in the knowledge that, if more were ahead for them, he would be there for her in a way she had never experienced with anyone else before.

That was a huge part of their earlier problem. After the death of her parents, everything had fallen on her shoulders, and she hadn't been prepared or trained in any way to handle the trauma of Kelly and her issues. With Jaxon deployed, instead of having somebody to turn to, she had pushed everyone away, including him, isolating herself.

With tears still in her eyes, she kissed every inch of him, smiling in joy at his soft groans of delight. Massaging, caressing every last inch of him until he couldn't stand it anymore, she soon found herself flipped onto her back.

He growled at her. "You think you'll just keep teasing me?"

She giggled. "No, yet it seems I had forgotten so much, and there is joy in discovering all the little nooks and crannies that you loved to have touched."

He smiled and nodded. "Remember though that two can play that game." Then he proceeded to go over every inch of her, until she was crying out and begging for him to stop.

When he finally shifted and slid into position, she groaned, wrapped her thighs around his hips, and plunged upward, meeting him with every ounce of her being, as he drove home. With his last surge, she came apart in joy, feeling it spread through her heart and her soul, until she was gasping in absolute delight at everything that had just happened between them.

When he slipped off to her side and pulled her into his arms, he whispered, "Are you okay?"

She rolled her head sideways to smile at him. "I can hardly breathe, but the answer is absolutely."

He smiled and hugged her. "Good, now get some sleep."

She closed her eyes, tucked up against him, and, when her heart finally stilled, she drifted off into a light sleep.

When she woke a little bit later, he was holding her tight, whispering against her ear, "Don't move. We have a visitor. I'm keeping the dogs quiet, work to keep it that way. I want to know who this asshole is, not scare him off."

She opened her eyes and reared back. Both dogs were lying on the bed staring at the door, growling low and deep in their throats. She staring at him, but he held a finger against her lips, even as he grabbed his prosthetic and pulled it on.

She knew it couldn't be comfortable because he didn't add the sock first, but that wouldn't be his issue right now. He was bound and determined to get up and to deal with whatever threat was outside.

She quickly pulled on her nightie and stepped up beside him. Her hands on both dogs at her side. Moving forward as a team, he pulled her slowly and carefully toward the door, and then she heard the footsteps. The squeaky stairs were an issue her mother had always gone on about with her father, but he'd just smiled at her, saying, "There's a darn-good reason for having squeaky stairs."

Keisha had never really understood until she had been a teenager, and trying to sneak into her bedroom was a lost cause. She never could pull it off because invariably her father stood there in the hallway, that frown on his face, catching her. Maybe that happened with Kelly too, once Keisha had gone off to college. Even now, she realized that's exactly what those squeaky steps were for. Somebody was in her house and approaching them while they slept, and the only reason to be doing that was if they had nefarious intentions.

She looked over at Jaxon and whispered, "I don't have a weapon in the house."

He just nodded, and she frowned. When she went to open her mouth again, he shook his head. As the footsteps neared her bedroom door, he pulled her to the side of it, behind him, and just waited. The dogs strained, but thankfully seemed to understand. With her hand on both, she managed to keep them silent, but the ridges were high on their backs and both dogs looked ready to pounce.

The doorknob turned ever-so-slightly, making her eyes widen and her heart slam against her chest. She realized the intruder not only knew the layout of the house, but he also knew where she would be. And, with that, she realized the extent of Kelly's involvement yet again.

Feeling the pain of the betrayal and knowing she would have to deal with that later as well, the door was pushed open silently, but she couldn't see who it was yet. The room was dark.

When the intruder lifted his handgun, and several shots were fired into the bed, she cried out, unable to hold it back. Neither could she keep the dogs back. All hell broke loose at the dogs lunged and Jaxon slammed the door hard against the intruder, knocking the gun to the floor, as Jaxon grabbed the intruder's arm, flipped the man to the ground, and immediately stomped on his arm and pulled it backward. She barely heard the bone crack as the man screamed in pain, and the dogs barked and bit at what they could reach, and Jaxon was giving no quarter as he dropped down hard, his knees landing on the man's back. He roared to her, "Call Richard."

She immediately raced over to where she had plugged in her phone to recharge and placed the call. As she tried to explain, she was still frantic as she stared at the intruder.

Richard had to ask her to calm down.

"We have a gunman," she gasped. "A gunman came into my house. Just shot up my bed. Come right now … please."

"Are you okay?"

"We're okay. Jaxon's got him on the floor. He had a gun," she cried out. "He came in here with a weapon."

"I'm on my way, and I've got a police unit coming." He hesitated, then asked, "Is the intruder alive?"

"Yes, yes," she snapped, "but he'll need the goddamn hospital."

A note of humor was in his tone when Richard added, "I'm not entirely against that, but I don't want Jaxon to kill him," he stated firmly. "You keep him calm because chances are this guy is part of this whole Chat mess."

"I'm sure he is," she declared bitterly, "and he knew exactly which room to go to."

At that, Richard went silent and then added, "I'm sorry."

"Yeah, … me too." She sighed. "Me too."

"And again let's not jump to conclusions," he pointed out.

"I'm not jumping to anything," she stated in frustration

and anger. "But it's pretty-damn obvious how he found out exactly where to find me."

"And you're in the master bedroom, right?"

"Yes, but how did you know?"

"That's where it would make the most sense as to where you'd sleep."

"No, not when I have a sister who's in a wheelchair," she pointed out. "It would make more sense to have her in here, since it's larger and has the bathroom attached. The only reason I'm in the master is because it's upstairs, and Kelly can't get up here."

"Got it," he muttered. She heard a vehicle start up in the background. "The black-and-white is on its way," Richard announced, "and I am too."

"Sorry, I didn't mean to drag you out of bed."

He snorted. "Story of my life."

"Maybe, yet I just …"

"I know. I know. You want it all to go away."

"Yes, that's exactly what I want," she snapped, trying to still her shaking. "I'm not sure that'll be an option at this point."

"Let's just get to the bottom of this first."

When she disconnected, she shared, "Richard's on his way, along with a black-and-white. He said to tell you to not kill him. He added *please*."

Both dogs were milling around wanting to help but not knowing how. She loved their helpfulness, not to mention adding a bit of lightness to this crazy nightmare.

The man on the ground thrashed as if a fish out of water, and Jaxon pushed him back down to the floor. "I won't kill him," Jaxon replied, but then stomped the man in the back again. "Stop moving, or I might change my mind."

She looked down at the man, then her gaze went to the weapon sitting on the ground.

"Don't touch it. Leave it exactly where it is," Jaxon snapped.

"I need to unlock the door so they can get in, but I don't want to leave you with him."

He smiled at her and added, "If he moves, I'll break his other arm."

At that, the other man started swearing at him, cussing him out heavily, but she believed Jaxon. "Fine, but I want him to be conscious, so I can give him a good couple kicks myself," she snapped. "What an ass." She raced downstairs to unlock the front door, then bolted back upstairs again. She feared what she might find when she flew back into her bedroom, but nothing had changed. She closed her eyes and took several deep breaths.

Jaxon asked, "Now, do you want to get some clothes on?"

"I do." And then she giggled when she looked at him and asked, "What about you?"

He looked down at his nude body. "Not really much of an option until they get here," he shared, with a note of humor, "but I won't be embarrassed about it."

"Neither am I," she stated. "It's a hell of a view."

"Thank you."

"You're welcome," she whispered her grin widening.

"Do you guys mind?" the gunman snarled. "That's the last fucking thing I want to think about dangling above my head."

"That's your problem," she snapped, staring down at him, "and I sure hope he ruined your arm for life."

With that, he started to struggle again, and Jaxon immediately pushed on his broken arm ever-so-slightly, and the gunman started screaming at the top of his lungs. She barely heard the clambering and the commotions downstairs, but, when she did, she raced out to the top of the railing and yelled for the cops to come up. She was still pulling the t-shirt on over her head while they came barreling up the stairs. She had to secure the dogs in the bathroom as they went crazy barking at the new arrivals.

When they got upstairs, the gunman was still screaming and hollering like he'd been shot. She looked over at them and said, "He's fine, except for his arm." Then she pointed to the gun. "That's his."

The officers looked at her, considered the scenario, then one immediately went over and secured the weapon. He asked, "Did you guys get shot?"

She shook her head. "No, but I'm not so sure my bed will survive."

He immediately looked over at the bed, where it had obviously been shot several times, with feathers sticking out of pillows and damage elsewhere. He looked back at her, his eyebrows raised.

She added, "If you know Detective Richard Martin, this all has to do with a current case of his."

"I can check with him," the officer replied, and he turned to Jaxon. "Step back, please, and you may want to put some clothes on," he added, as he pointed at Jaxon's naked body.

"I'd be happy to," he muttered, with a smile, "but I would feel much better if you would secure him first."

"I can do that. Do I need to call Detective Martin, or is he on his way?"

"He's on his way," she added.

"Actually I'm right here," Richard said, from the doorway. He surveyed the mess and shook his head. "I'm really glad to see this guy is alive and still kicking," he noted, with a nod. He looked over at the cops. "Secure him, please, so we can get Jaxon up on his feet again."

And, with that, she turned to see the policeman quickly helping the gunman to his feet. He wasn't putting up much of a fight, his arm hanging at an odd angle and his face white.

Jaxon now stood awkwardly on his prosthetic, still not a stitch on his body, revealing a few others scars she was seeing for the very first time, now that a light was on. She walked over to her bathroom and grabbed a large bath towel for him.

He wrapped it around his body, then looked at the gunman. "That piece of shit came right up the stairs, walked straight through to the master bedroom, opened the door, and started firing into the bed."

Richard nodded. "Obviously you heard him coming, I presume." He looked from one to the other.

She smiled. "My father intentionally left a few squeaky stairs, something my mother was always on him to fix. He never would do it, and it wasn't until I was a teenager and got caught sneaking home late that I realized why. And now I find myself forever grateful for his foresight."

"Of course," Richard agreed, "that's a smart dad." He grinned and added, "With two daughters, a very smart dad."

She rolled her eyes at that. "Oh, please, I highly doubt that sons are any better."

"No, but dads don't seem to care about them as much," he explained, with a laugh. He looked over at Jaxon and pointed. "You need to get that prosthetic off and put it on properly or it'll be sore as hell tomorrow. The last thing you need is an infection, and you've probably already got bruising. Get yourselves dressed, and I'll talk to you downstairs."

"What will you do now?" she asked.

"We'll get forensics in here. They will retrieve the bullets and take a bunch of photos, not to mention anything else they might find, like fingerprints."

"He's got gloves on," she noted, "so I don't think fingerprints will be an issue."

"Maybe not," he conceded, "but we'll do the full workup, including printing the inside of those gloves."

She nodded, and, as soon as he disappeared, Jaxon made his way over to the bed and managed to get his prosthetic off. She could see that it hurt him to do it, but then he proceeded to put it on properly. She grabbed some jeans and quickly dressed, and, by the time they were ready to go downstairs, she grabbed up leashes, brought the dogs out from the bathroom and they headed straight to the kitchen and put on coffee. Then opened the back kitchen door and let the dogs out into the fenced yard. It was a lot of excitement for them too.

She checked her watch. It was three in the morning, but she also knew that this would go on for several more hours now. She groaned as she walked back into the living room. "Does that mean the harassment is over now?"

"I would think so, though I wasn't expecting this part of it," Richard admitted, turning to look at her. "And I don't think you were either."

"No, not at all," she admitted, with a shiver. "I was really hoping that we were done when my sister confessed about whatever the hell she was involved in."

"Now we'll have another talk with Kelly," Richard declared.

Keisha grimaced, then nodded. "I have no desire to be there for that one."

"No, and you don't have to," he confirmed, with a nod. "But you might want to consider that, if she did tell them about the house and about where you were sleeping, she did *not* tell them about the squeaky steps."

She stopped at that and looked over at him, feeling something settle in her heart. "Thank you for that reminder," she muttered. "I'll just wait until I hear what she has to say."

He nodded approvingly. "Good idea."

A few minutes later she sat down cups of coffee for everybody. She looked over at Jaxon and muttered, "I'm really hoping I can get back to sleep tonight."

He laughed. "Depends on how much coffee you have."

As it was, it didn't take very long to go over the events, and, when Richard was finally done, he said, "Do not contact Kelly right now, please. I want to talk to her first."

"Of course," Keisha agreed. "What are you looking for?"

"I'm hoping that something in here proves she's not involved. I don't know whether the gunman came here tonight because we're working to shut down that group or what. Maybe somebody figured out the info on the group came from Kelly. Again, I don't know. But you talking to her won't help and could possibly hinder my investigation, so I want to speak to her first."

"In that case," she noted, looking shocked, "somebody needs to confirm she's okay at the hospital."

"That is a consideration, and I'm heading over there right now," Richard confirmed. "I don't think that will be a concern, since you were the ones who were threatened, not her."

"No, not her, not here, but, if she gave something away about the Chat group, maybe revenge is just how they operate."

"Maybe," Richard muttered, then he stood up. "I'll let you know, but please don't contact her." And, with that, he and the cops were gone.

She looked over at Jaxon. "Do you think Kelly's safe there?"

"I would think so, especially since she's under constant suicide watch. Still, it's good that Richard's headed over there too. It could be that our gunman had a partner, but I don't think so. As far as the police are concerned, one man is behind this."

"Sure, but that doesn't mean he isn't getting other people to do his crap. As we already know, they want to get others involved."

"That's true, but we will wait and see. Richard's driving to the hospital right now."

She sat here, finished her coffee, which was surprisingly good considering the hour, and then she muttered, "I don't even know if I can sleep again."

"It's almost four now," he pointed out, "and you probably need more sleep. You didn't sleep that much, especially considering the fact that we didn't exactly make good use of the sleep time that we had earlier."

She snickered. "I think we made the best use possible," she countered, with a grin on her face. "I'm certainly not regretting it."

"Good, but by this afternoon you might be feeling differently."

"I'll have a nap, remember?"

"And what about the llamas?"

She looked at him and laughed, then added, "I could always go lie down on a hay bale and have a nap there. Who knows? … It could be fun."

"That's not a bad idea," he agreed, with a grin. As he tossed back the last of his coffee, he added, "I still suggest we at least try to get some sleep."

And, with that, he let the dogs back in and led all of them back upstairs—but to the spare bedroom this time.

CHAPTER 24

JAXON AND KEISHA woke later in the morning, and he quickly organized a quick meal for them. Then they headed to Timber's place, Harley and Homer happily seated in the back seat.

When they got there, Timber stepped out on the front steps. "Hey, you two. I've already talked to Richard this morning. Sounds as if you had one hell of a night. And Kelly remains safe at the hospital."

"Oh, good," Keisha exclaimed. "I was about to call to check on her."

Jaxon shook his head. "It's been a hell of a couple days."

"I hear that. Are you back to visit?" Timber asked.

"Back to visit, to keep working, and to sort out what's going on that we don't already know," he shared, waving his hands awkwardly, trying hard to stay off his leg that was chaffing him. "I'm still planning on showing up every day." He could see the unmistakable relief on Timber's face. "I'm not bailing on you, so don't worry about that."

"Hey, everybody needs to bail when they need to bail," Timber said easily. "It's just hard when everything is related to the assholes in this world instead of progress around here. And, man oh man, will my project manager be on our case if she thinks we're about to lose people. Prioritizing and staying on schedule is huge, apparently."

Jaxon grinned. "You and I both know Shirley is doing an amazing job keeping you organized. You wouldn't know your ass from your foot."

Timber sighed. "Yeah, I know it. It never occurred to me that I needed a professional organizer. Or a Project Manager, according to her." He grinned at that. "But apparently, once things blew up, they blew up in a bad way."

"But for all the right reasons," he pointed out.

Timber waved him in. "Come on inside. Get some coffee," he offered.

Keisha interjected, "We have a bunch of llamas that I'm hoping to check over today."

"I've got a paddock ready for them, and they're still separate from the horses. Once you check them out, then we'll see how they do with the horses."

"They generally do quite well with horses," Keisha offered, "but it often depends on the horses."

"So far, there doesn't seem to be anything untoward happening across the fence, but you don't know for sure until you try to mix them together," Timber noted. "So we'll keep the alpacas separate for a day or two more. Meanwhile, come give us your best guess with the llamas."

"Will do," she said. "Are we taking coffee with us, or coming back for it afterward? Not to mention I have feed for the llamas that needs to be unloaded too."

"I'll get one of the guys to unload the feed. And if you need a coffee, go grab a mug," he offered. "I guess you haven't had a whole lot of sleep, have you?"

"No, I sure haven't," she admitted. "I'll go until I can't go anymore, and then I've already threatened to drop onto a hay bale and have a nap, if need be. We do what we have to."

He burst out laughing at that. "I'm pretty sure we have

more comfortable accommodations around there. There's a couch, plus a spare bed upstairs," he shared, with a grin. "So, if you find you need a nap, by all means, take one."

"Is Tiffany here?"

"Nope, she's at the clinic."

Keisha nodded, and they headed over to the paddocks with the llamas. As soon as she walked up, several of the llamas walked over, looking for attention. She smiled, noting that they seemed to be adjusting well to the temperatures, since they'd been shorn. They were all looking quite a bit better.

She checked several hooves, took their temperatures, and, with a nod, indicated her satisfaction with their condition. "They're all good." And, with that, Timber opened up one of the side gates, and the llamas, though hesitant at first, quickly gained confidence and raced out into the much bigger space. They all laughed as the animals kicked up their heels and thundered around and around the pasture.

She looked over at Timber. "I was speaking to one of my suppliers yesterday, and they're interested in giving you a hand with feed."

Timber raised his eyebrows at her and smiled. "I'll never say no to that. Hopefully it's a different one than we're already connected with. Keeping these guys fed will be an interesting challenge moving forward."

"Exactly, particularly if you want to do any advertising for this group."

"What kind of advertising?" he asked warily.

She shrugged. "No clue, but possibly a sticker on your truck won't be a problem, is it?"

"No, I can handle that much," he said, waving his

hands. "However, I sure won't get into that social media crap," he declared, with a snort.

"I don't think that's required," she added, with a chuckle. "Definitely not your thing, *huh*?"

"No. … It'll never be my thing," he snapped, with another snort. "So, if they are looking for that, they can go find somebody else."

"Nope, that's not their thing either, but they're happy to help. When I explained what you had going on here, they were pretty impressed at the scope of what you're working with. They just know that you'll need a hand."

"I'll take all the help I can get," he admitted, "so thank you for that."

And, with that, she smiled. They were just getting ready to head back to the main cabin for more coffee when her phone rang. She glanced at it, then looked back at Jaxon. "It's Richard."

"Good," He stepped up closer, and she put it on Speaker. "I'm here with Jaxon and Timber," Keisha shared, looking back and forth between them. "So, what's the update?"

"Kelly says that she did give them the address, but then realized they were getting more and more aggressive about it and got scared, but she never really thought they would come and hurt you. When I told her that you survived the shooting, she broke down into tears again, saying she was the worst person ever. She did say that it seemed as if, once she started down the road with this group, it just snowballed. Yet she was so full of anger and hurt that she didn't know how to get out of it or even see that she needed to."

"So, she was sucked in, with no way out. Is that what's she claiming?" Jaxon asked hotly.

Richard replied, "Do I think that she thought Keisha would be injured or killed? No, … I don't. Do I think that she thought they would hassle you guys some more? … Yes, and she was all for it."

"So, it's not a defense on her part."

"Yes and no," Richard clarified. "Kelly was up to her neck in it, but they crossed the line, … a line she didn't even see coming."

Keisha closed her eyes and pinched the bridge of her nose. "Dear God, what a shitshow."

"I know," Richard noted. "It's a bit much to take in. Because of all that and the suicide attempt, Kelly won't be free anytime soon. She'll go to an institute to be evaluated, based on what she's done to herself and to you. Meanwhile, I'll talk to my captain and the district attorney to see just what we're looking at with the fraud issue."

"Good, she needs all the help she can get too," Jaxon stated, as Keisha busily pushed back her tears.

Richard added, "On a positive note, we were able to get some information from the man you guys captured in your house last night. We've located several other men involved, including the ringleader."

"That's great news."

"He's not in the state, but he is in the country, so we have a warrant out for his arrest right now. Last I heard, the feds would head right out and try to pick him up at his home, which would effectively shut down this online Chat group."

"Now that is good news," Keisha exclaimed in delight. "I would absolutely love to think that he could be in custody and shut down."

"Oh, it'll be more than shut down. There will also be a

very large investigation, specifically looking into the deaths of people who were part of the group. This guy specializes in pushing people to kill themselves," Richard explained, "and, while that's a concept many of us just can't comprehend, for him, it's become a way of life and is how he gains power over his situation. He's apparently also in a wheelchair but loves to power-trip. Also, if you were dead, then Kelly would get everything, which she would then be pressured to share with the group, as she has already been doing."

"Good God, that's awful."

"I know," Richard agreed. "Another one for the psychologists to study but not your problem anymore. You guys are free and clear, so maybe you should take some time and just relax a bit. As far as Kelly, I don't know what will end up happening, but she won't be going anywhere for quite a while."

"No, I understand that …"

"Also, it's probably not what you want to hear, but she doesn't want to see you."

"No, of course not, and I can respect that. At the same time, it would be nice if I could see her one more time before she goes."

"She has not agreed to that," Richard stated firmly, "so please don't ask because I can't allow it. She's not in the right state of mind for you to be confronting her."

"Right, and that's fine," she agreed. "I can honor that request. It doesn't matter, and I guess I can see where she's coming from. If that's what she wants, then that's what she wants."

"She'll probably do some healing and be able to talk to you later," Richard offered, "but, for the moment, I highly suggest you just move forward and heal your own life. And sort out your funds. She gave away a lot of your money, so that needs replacing. I can see about the total figures on all that, see what the credit card companies have decided to do, and, if she's charged, it will be easier for them to write it off."

"*Right*," Keisha replied, rolling her eyes.

"We do need you to come in and sign your statements."

"Sometime tomorrow, maybe?" she asked, with a questioning look over at Jaxon. "I have the clinic open all day tomorrow, but I can run over on my lunch hour. Eva and Tania can cover for me a bit, if need be."

"That'll be good," Richard said. "We'll have it all written up. I just want to confirm that it's all clear and what you want to say."

"Can you email it to me?" she asked. "That way, we can make any edits needed, then come in just to sign."

"Sounds good," he said.

With that, she disconnected and looked over at the other two men. "I can't even imagine," she muttered, "and right now my sister has got to be feeling terrible."

"I'm sure she is," Jaxon agreed, with a nod. "Yet …"

"I know," she said, holding up a hand.

Timber nodded. "She brought this on herself, but you can't overlook her mental state, so thankfully she'll be getting the help that she needs now," Timber stated. "There will be a future for her—though we don't know what that'll look like. It doesn't even matter right now, but hopefully she'll turn a corner and begin to heal."

"I hope so," Keisha whispered.

"Timber is right, as usual," Jaxon declared. "Always the voice of reason. It seems she got herself on such a rough road, but she put herself there, and now she'll have the opportunity to do the work to get herself out."

Keisha frowned. "Richard never mentioned anything about any charges related to the car accident."

"The weather conditions still played a huge role, so they'll probably leave it at that," Jaxon guessed, looking at her. "She admitted it herself. The weather conditions were terrible, and she didn't have the experience to handle them. Apparently, a lot of accidents happened that night."

"Right," she muttered. "That would be a blessing if they just left it alone."

"Not so much for the other family though."

She winced. "The expanding circles of people affected by everything in life are always there, aren't they?"

"Yes," Jaxon stated, as Timber nodded. "You know that theory about six degrees of separation?"

"Yeah," she replied, "but you don't really think about it until something like this happens."

"And now you don't need to think about it all," Jaxon declared. He turned her so she was looking back at the llamas, who were still racing around the pasture, kicking up their heels. "This is what we get to focus on now. Helping other animals and people find the life they deserve."

She looked over at Timber and nodded. "You've really created an absolutely beautiful sanctuary here, and the Haven is a perfect name. The animals will appreciate it so much."

Timber walked over, slung an arm over her shoulders, and gave her a quick hug. "It's not just for animals, you know? You're welcome anytime."

"Wait until you meet Big Mike," Jaxon teased, with a chuckle.

"Who is that?" she asked.

Timber smiled and looked out at the acres that surrounded him. "Big Mike is a very old, very tired, very worn-out bear that comes and goes as he pleases. And you haven't seen the huge owl named Gibraltar yet. Or the bobcat. … There is so much more to see here if you hang around long enough."

Jaxon and Timber both grinned from ear to ear.

She smiled broadly. "I can't wait."

EPILOGUE

Several Weeks Later ...

TIMBER WALKED OUT onto the deck. It was only 5:30 in the morning, yet Toby and Dwight were already up and sitting outside, a cup of coffee in their hands.

Dwight asked Timber, "How is the coyote that came in yesterday?"

"I haven't looked at him yet this morning," Timber replied, "but he was the last thing I checked on last night. He'll lose part of that leg, but I think he'll adapt, as he's pretty young."

"He's just a pup, isn't he?"

"I think so, maybe four months or so. Tiffany wasn't exactly sure. She will try to bring Keisha out to take a look at him today."

"That'll be good. I'm sure she'll come out pretty much every day she's not working at her clinic."

"She's welcome to do just that," Timber stated, with a sigh. "She's not charging me for her services, so God knows she's welcome to come help anytime." He took a chair beside Toby.

"You're doing good things here, boss."

Dwight nodded in agreement.

Timber snorted. "I still don't know how I ended up with all I ended up with and so fast," he admitted, shaking his head. "So many people still work here, making things happen. Just trying to keep an eye on all the projects, not to mention the scheduling and management of everything else, is a hell of a job in itself."

"Which is a good thing, especially now that you have somebody to look after it," Toby pointed out.

"Shirley is a great help, but let's face it, Toby. I'm not paying her or anybody else, including you. That can't go on much longer."

"No, but right now that's not an issue."

Timber sighed. "I come from a world where, if you do a job, you expect to get paid."

"And yet what about you? You're trying to set up something to help animals, so when do you get paid? Maybe what you need to do is find a way to make some money off your rescue organization. I don't have any suggestions as to that part," Toby began, then chuckled. "However, with all the land you've got here, what about boarding horses?"

Timber looked over at him. "You mean, that dozen we've got isn't enough?"

"No, not considering you've got room here for hundreds," he replied, with a smile. "We would have to set it up properly, but it would be a good source of income, and an awful lot of people want to keep their horses nearby but don't have the land for them."

"We're a little out of the way for that, aren't we?" Timber asked, with a sigh.

"Sure, but it's not too far from town, and we already know that horses absolutely love being here. But the good part is that it would give us some income. The other thing I was thinking about was dog boarding, you know, like for vacations."

At that, Timber immediately nodded. "I was going to mention that myself," he muttered.

"I think that's pretty good money, and you've definitely got the space," Toby noted, circling his arm. "I think you could do a lot with that idea. And then, of course, you've been talking all along about training some animals."

"I wanted to train some therapy animals, for sure," he agreed, "and maybe some other canine specialties, depending on who and what comes along. I'm particularly talking about K9 training to locate contraband, for airports and the like."

"That would be great, but do you have any experience with it?"

"I have some, but, better still, an old K9-training buddy of mine reached out, and he's just come out of rehab. Sounds as if he's a little lost."

"That seems to be a perfect answer for him and for the Haven," Toby said. "Who is it?"

"His name is Sterling." Timber laughed. "Good memories there. He's been training animals for airports and for the police, really all kinds of specialty work, depending on what the animal showed an inclination for. He's been working on helping identify and increase their training abilities, so I was wondering about that."

"That sounds great."

Timber added, "I hesitate to even bring this up, but you did hear a rescue in town needs help?"

Toby nodded. "I wondered if they would contact you at some point."

"Yeah, they've asked me about, ... are you ready? Fifty dogs. They've just gotten dogs from a puppy mill breeder that was shut down. Among the fifty are something like thirty-two puppies and maybe eight nursing mothers."

Toby just stared at him, then shook his head. "Good thing you got the extra acreage, I guess. You'll need to get set up to recover the cost of caring for these animals in the adoption fee. You know, the cost of the care and the cost of finding them good decent homes. You'll also need somebody who can keep track of that too."

He snorted. "That'll require somebody with good organization and clerical abilities. I would suggest Shirley do it, but I'm afraid she's got enough to keep track of as it is. I sure don't want to run her off."

"Maybe this Sterling has somebody in mind."

Timber shrugged. "The rescue did say they had somebody coming over to check out the Haven's surroundings today. I didn't give them a time. I just told them to pop on by whenever and explained how we were all still really busy building the needed structures around here. She seemed quite impressed. So anyway we can expect to see someone named Lindsey Sagwey come by today," he shared.

"Good, and when is Sterling coming?" Toby asked.

"He took a bus, arriving in town today. So, I thought I would run in and pick him up. Plus, I can go grab feed and anything else we need."

"Sounds good," Dwight agreed, with a nod. "Have him here for lunch, and he'll get to know everybody real fast."

"That's what I was thinking," Timber murmured. "He's a big man, but he's one of those huge gentle-giant types," he said. "And animals of all kinds seem to love him."

"There you go. Looks as if he'll fit right in. How many individual properties do we have lined up?" Big Toby asked, lost in thought. "At the rate we're going, you could end up needing quite a few of them."

"We have twelve at the moment," Timber replied. "I'm

not sure on the rest of that."

"You know that Dwight and I want our two," Toby reminded him. "So any time you're ready to start designing them, we'll start surveying the property."

Timber frowned at him. "Yeah, Dwight, you're a surveyor, aren't you?"

"Yeah, why?"

"That would be perfect," he muttered, and then he laughed. "I swear to God. … I started to build a rescue, and I feel as if we're building a town or something."

Toby turned to him, shaking his head. "No, not at all. You built a community, dude. This is a rescue, but it's more than that. True to its name, it's a haven for all of us, … animals and people alike."

This concludes Book 3 of The Haven: Jaxon.
Read about Sterling: The Haven, Book 4

The Haven: Sterling (Book #4)

For Sterling, encountering Toby and the others at the Haven feels like a glimpse of redemption. He is adrift, trapped between the shadows of his past and the foggy uncertainty of his present. The proximity to his mother's farm, now under his aunt's control, only heightens his unease. Many years ago she had cast him into the foster system, and now he faces a choice: continue on in silence or confront the storm brewing dangerously close. Does he really want to fully engage in this looming conflict and to stand firm to the end? Doesn't he have enough on this plate already?

Lindsay arrives at the Haven with cautious hope, seeking to verify its promise. She is no stranger to the struggles of small rescues, and the possibility of a new ally offers a glimmer of relief. Meeting Sterling—and realizing he might be the cousin her friend had never known—adds layers of complexity to the situation. The revelation of his tangled past and the simmering current tensions only deepens the intrigue.

The impending clash promises to be brutal, and, as the

stakes rise, two questions linger. Who would emerge unscathed? And could love find a way amid the chaos?

Find Book 4 here!

To find out more visit Dale Mayer's website.

https://geni.us/DMSTHSterling

Author's Note

Thank you for reading Jaxon: The Haven, Book 3! If you enjoyed the book, please take a moment and leave a short review.

Dear reader,

I love to hear from readers, and you can contact me at my website: www.dalemayer.com or at my Facebook author page. To be informed of new releases and special offers, sign up for my newsletter or follow me on BookBub. And if you are interested in joining Dale Mayer's Reader Group, here is the Facebook sign up page.
http://geni.us/DaleMayerFBGroup

Cheers,
Dale Mayer

About the Author

Dale Mayer is a *USA Today* best-selling author, best known for her SEALs military romances, her Psychic Visions series, and her Lovely Lethal Garden cozy series. Her contemporary romances are raw and full of passion and emotion (Broken But … Mending, Hathaway House series). Her thrillers will keep you guessing (Kate Morgan, By Death series), and her romantic comedies will keep you giggling (*It's a Dog's Life*, a stand-alone novella; and the Broken Protocols series, starring Charming Marvin, the cat).

Dale honors the stories that come to her—and some of them are crazy, break all the rules and cross multiple genres!

To go with her fiction, she also writes nonfiction in many different fields, with books available on résumé writing, companion gardening, and the US mortgage system. All her books are available in print and ebook format.

Connect with Dale Mayer Online

Dale's Website – www.dalemayer.com
Twitter – @DaleMayer
Facebook Page – geni.us/DaleMayerFBFanPage
Facebook Group – geni.us/DaleMayerFBGroup
BookBub – geni.us/DaleMayerBookbub
Instagram – geni.us/DaleMayerInstagram
Goodreads – geni.us/DaleMayerGoodreads
Newsletter – geni.us/DaleNews